IT LOOKED LIKE
AN EASY ASSIGNMENT . . .

"Here's some mail that arrived for Mary Yates after she moved. I haven't been sure whether I should open it or not."

I took the two envelopes and opened them. One was from a local department store, advising Mary Yates that her check had bounced. The other was from Las Vegas, a woman who signed herself "Aunt Mae."

"I don't usually commit felonies, Mrs. Halliday," I replied to the slightly shocked look on her face. "Only when I think it may help. What about the car?"

She gave me a description of the car. A late-model Oldsmobile, white with red interior. "Are you sure you can handle this?" she said. "They might not want to give up the car."

"I'm sure I can handle it. And if I need help, I'll get it. I don't have a macho image to maintain."

MORE MYSTERIES FROM THE
BERKLEY PUBLISHING GROUP . . .

INSPECTOR KENWORTHY MYSTERIES: Scotland Yard's consummate master of investigation lets no one get away with murder. "In the best tradition of British detective fiction!"—*Boston Globe*

by John Buxton Hilton

HANGMAN'S TIDE
FATAL CURTAIN
PLAYGROUND OF DEATH

CRADLE OF CRIME
HOLIDAY FOR MURDER
DEAD MAN'S PATH

DOG LOVER'S MYSTERIES STARRING JACKIE WALSH: She's starting a new life with her son and an ex-police dog named Jake . . . teaching film classes and solving crimes!

by Melissa Cleary

A TAIL OF TWO MURDERS

GARTH RYLAND MYSTERIES: Newsman Garth Ryland digs up the dirt in a serene small town—that isn't as peaceful as it looks . . . "A writer with real imagination!"—*The New York Times*

by John R. Riggs

HUNTING GROUND
HAUNT OF THE NIGHTINGALE

PETER BRICHTER MYSTERIES: A midwestern police detective stars in "a highly unusual, exceptionally erudite mystery series!"—*Minneapolis Star Tribune*

by Mary Monica Pulver

KNIGHT FALL
THE UNFORGIVING MINUTES

ASHES TO ASHES
ORIGINAL SIN

TEDDY LONDON MYSTERIES: A P.I. solves mysteries with a touch of the supernatural . . .

by Robert Morgan

THE THINGS THAT ARE NOT THERE

JACK HAGEE, P.I. MYSTERIES: Classic detective fiction with "raw vitality . . . Henderson is a born storyteller."—*Armchair Detective*

by C.J. Henderson

NO FREE LUNCH

FREDDIE O'NEAL, P.I. MYSTERIES: You can bet that this appealing Reno P.I. will get her man . . . "A winner."—Linda Grant

by Catherine Dain

LAY IT ON THE LINE

SISTER FREVISSE MYSTERIES: Medieval mystery in the tradition of Ellis Peters . . .

by Margaret Frazer

THE NOVICE'S TALE

LAY IT ON THE LINE

CATHERINE DAIN

JOVE BOOKS, NEW YORK

LAY IT ON THE LINE

A Jove Book / published by arrangement with
the author

PRINTING HISTORY
Jove edition / September 1992

ISBN: 0-515-10926-6

Jove Books are published by The Berkley Publishing Group,
200 Madison Avenue, New York, New York 10016.
The name ''JOVE'' and the ''J'' logo
are trademarks belonging to Jove Publications, Inc.

For Paul Dain
who had the technical expertise

I never lay my money on the line until I understand clearly the game I'm going to play.

—Harold S. Smith, Sr.
I Want to Quit Winners

Chapter

1

AS THE CATERPILLAR said to Alice (at least I think it was the Caterpillar—I didn't look it up), it's best to begin at the beginning. In this case, a sweltering August afternoon. I had just come back to my office after having lunch at the coffee shop of the Mother Lode Casino (what I had for lunch was disappointment—I lost four Keno games in a row), cleaned up the remains of a half-eaten sparrow, and decided the few small jobs I had hanging could wait while I spent the rest of the afternoon sitting in front of a fan shooting down computerized Klingons, when the phone rang. A woman's voice asked if I was available, said she wanted to hire me for what she hoped was a simple task. I hesitated long enough to let her think I might be busy, then suggested three o'clock. I finished the game before she arrived.

She was tall and beautiful, and she strode into my office as if she owned the building, not that it was much of a building to own. The casual drape of her full-skirted white dress softened the angles of her shoulders and made her tan luminous. Her hair was a blond halo, and only the fine lines around her eyes and the blue shadows beyond covering hinted that she was on the downhill side of forty. Or maybe it was just that I knew who she was. Her name was Joan Halliday, and she had been the captain of the chorus line at the old Sierra Madre Casino for years. I remembered how I had loved to watch her dance, how much I had envied her, how much I had wanted to look like her when I grew up. I don't. I have blond hair, but there the resemblance ends. Mine is long and coarse and streaked, and about all I ever do with it is brush it into a rubber band at the nape of my neck.

"Thank you for waiting," she said as she arranged herself in the canvas chair beside my desk.

"No problem. As you can see, home isn't far. And I don't really keep regular hours anyway." My office is actually the living room of my house. In fact, I own the building.

I sat down in the old leather chair behind my desk, folded my hands, and waited while she rummaged through some papers in her large white handbag.

"Terry Dickerson recommended you," she told me as she rummaged.

I nodded. She had said that over the phone. Terry Dickerson was a real estate agent who hired me occasionally for skip-trace work.

"I hadn't expected Freddie O'Neal to be a woman."

I waited for the stale joke about how my father must have wanted a boy, but she didn't make it.

"Why not?" I asked. "Terry's a pretty sensitive guy."

"Yes. I just didn't think of a woman doing this work."

"We're doing all kinds of things these days," I said, for probably the third time that week and the three thousandth in my career, smiling as reassuringly as I could.

"All right," she said, her patrician mouth almost smiling back as she put a small stack of papers on the desk. "Here's the situation. I came up here last week—I live in Las Vegas now—to help my sister move our father to a nursing home. It was the first time I had been here in a while, and—I hadn't realized, I had thought my sister was checking up on him—" She closed her eyes for a moment and then continued. "The house he had been living in, a rented house, had been trashed. It looked as if animals had been living there. There were stains on the walls, stains on the carpet, both food and what appears to be human waste. I told the woman who was supposed to be taking care of him that she had to get out, both she and her boyfriend, who had been staying with them. She had told my father that the boyfriend was her brother. She refused. She said they had permission to be in the house—my father had said they could—until the end of the month, two days ago. He also said they could use his car to get moved. Now they're gone, with the car, the house is almost demolished, and I want you to find them."

"Have you talked with the police?"

"Yes, but they say it's a civil matter because the woman had permission to be in the house and permission to take the car. The only thing we can do is take her to court for the damages—but we have to find her first."

"And you want me to find her."

"I want you to find her, pick up my father's car, and let me know if you see any sign of assets we could sue her for, to pay for the damages to the house. Although I don't expect there are any."

"I charge forty an hour, plus expenses, and I want you to be aware I might need to spend a little time riding around looking for that car."

"That's fine. Do you want money now?"

"No, that's okay. I can bill you. What information have you got for me?"

"The woman's name is Mary Yates. Her boyfriend is Willie Carver. The woman's daughter, Stephanie Johnson, came by periodically to borrow money. Neither my father nor my sister knows where she lives. Here is some mail that arrived for Mary Yates after she moved. I haven't been sure whether I should open it or not."

"Did you check with the post office to see if she left a forwarding address?"

"No."

I took the two envelopes and opened them. One was from a local department store, advising Mary Yates that her check had bounced. The other was from Las Vegas, a woman who signed herself "Aunt Mae."

"I don't usually commit felonies, Mrs. Halliday," I replied to the slightly shocked look on her face. "Only when I think it may help. What about the car?"

She gave me a description of the car. A late-model Oldsmobile, white with red interior. Not well cared for.

"One more question," I said when she was through. "Where does your sister come in? Since she's the one who lives in Reno, why isn't she taking care of this?"

Her mouth pursed, as if she had just bitten into an overripe fig and had no place to spit it.

"My sister isn't handling this very well. She has a bad case of white liberal guilt, and thinks we should just let them go, car and all."

"They're black?"

"Yes."

I nodded. "How can I get in touch with you?"

"I'm staying at the Bonanza Inn for the next few days. I'll let you know before I leave. Are you sure you can handle this? They might not want to give up the car."

"I'm sure I can handle it. And if I need help, I'll get it. I don't have a macho image to maintain."

She almost smiled again as she got up to leave. I followed her to the door.

"Mrs. Halliday?"

She paused, and I got embarrassed at what I was about to ask.

"How's Mick? He taught me to swim when I was eight years old, and I had a terrible crush on him." I blurted it out in one breath.

She was momentarily disconcerted, but then she laughed.

"He's fine. I'm sure he'll be pleased that you remember him fondly."

"Thank you."

Mick Halliday had been the lifeguard at the Sierra Madre Hotel swimming pool. I could remember how stunned my parents were when Joan Barrington married him and took a job as a dancer. I was too young to be stunned. And to me, Joan and Mick seemed like the perfect couple, both with movie-star looks. The fairy tale was even better because Joan's father, Charlie Barrington, owned the big hotel-casino right across the street.

Probably Charlie Barrington didn't think so. He had come to Reno right after World War II, the boomtown days, and opened a small casino called Charlie's Club. Twenty years later, the Barrington Hotel-Casinos in Reno and Stateline were the biggest employers in the state. Of course, that was when Reno was still the Biggest Little City in the World, where even casinos were kind of warm and folksy, in the years before water problems and sewer problems and smog problems, before the Bally and the MGM Grand recarved the face of northern Nevada into one less of dude ranches and divorcees than smooth, impersonal Las Vegas North.

As I remembered the local folklore, Charlie had had two daughters, Joan and Lois, by his first wife, whom he divorced shortly before he went big-time. She sued him for more money, but he countersued for custody of the girls, which he got, and cut her off with nothing. He played around for a number of years and then married again, a starlet close to his daughters' ages. There were some bad investments, some worse speculations, including a couple of movies starring his wife, and Charlie ended up in bankruptcy court. He wrote his autobiography, *The Roll of the Dice,* and made enough to keep himself off welfare. But he never came back. And now he was in a nursing home.

Lois, the older daughter, had married a history professor from the University of Nevada. A nice man, if a bit dull. Uninspiring. I had taken a required course in Western Civ from him. And Joan had lived her fairy-tale life—or so I imagined—with the handsome Mick Halliday.

I looked back at the papers on my desk. She had left a set of car keys and a letter authorizing me to take the car. There wasn't anything I could do before morning. Then I could start with the usual stuff. The post office, the DMV, the city directory, the bank where her check bounced. I had a friend with the Department of Social Services who could let me know if any of them had applied for unemployment or welfare. And if none of that panned out, I would ask a Las Vegas PI who was on my computer network to stop by and see Aunt Mae.

I locked the outside door to the office and turned out the lights. Joan Halliday's visit had made me aware of how dingy it was, how little I had done with it. The steel desk, the leather chair behind it, and the canvas chairs across from it were all scavenged from a garage sale. As was the table the computer and printer occupied. The overflowing bookcase had been in my bedroom when I was a kid. The walls sported a corkboard dotted with scraps of paper and an old Union Pacific poster. That was it.

The part of the house where I lived wasn't a lot better. Since the office should have been the living/dining room, I used one of the two small bedrooms for what it was intended and the other for everything else. The cats had used the sofa for a scratching post almost as many years as I had eaten dinner on it watching television. I try to be neat, but sometimes things spill. My latest attempts at greenery were dying in their plastic pots. And there was dust. I didn't have to check. I knew there was dust. Sometimes I thought about hiring someone to come in and clean, but I hadn't gotten around to it.

My bed wasn't made, dirty dishes clogged the kitchen sink, dirty clothes overflowed the hamper in the bathroom, the tile was mildewed, and the toothpaste was sitting on the edge of the bathroom basin, minus its cap. I didn't have to check that, either.

The yellow frame house sat in the southeast corner of downtown Reno, close enough to be zoned for business, and in fact not far from the police station. The area had never been a preferred residential zone—it used to be a red-light district—and even though the cat houses had by now moved out of the county, the neighborhood wasn't exactly classy. I hoped Joan Halliday would pay me enough to compensate for this unwanted insight into my own life.

My own cats—the other kind—two domestic longhairs, Butch and Sundance, one gray and white and the other orange—demanded food. I checked the refrigerator, and since there was food for them but not much for me, I took care of them and decided to walk to the Mother Lode for dinner, something I do altogether too often.

Reno is right at the edge of the great desert that covers most of the country between the Rockies and the Sierras, and no matter how warm it is during the day, the air cools rapidly when the sun goes down. So even though the day had been hot enough to mummify anyone fool enough to step out of the air-conditioning, I grabbed a denim jacket before I left the house. I was wearing a brown and white checked western-cut shirt, jeans, and boots. It may sound a little romantic that I like western-cut shirts, but my body is cut tall and angular, and I look as good in western shirts and jeans as in anything else. Besides, when you dress western, you never need to worry about whether it's in fashion. In Reno, it always is.

I hit Virginia Street and turned right. What had been the Sierra Madre was across the street, now refurbished with twice as much casino space and no showroom. The Barrington Hotel was still closed. I had read that it had been bought by some Japanese investors and would reopen in the fall.

I walked on up to where the street was nothing but flashing neon and turned into the Mother Lode, passing over the air grates that substituted for doors. When you never close, you don't need doors. Or clocks. Only heating and air-conditioning.

The comforting thunk of slot machine arms rippled around me like waves in a tidal pool as I moved toward the escalator to the coffee shop. I sat down at the counter, exchanged pleasantries with Diane, the waitress who always worked that section, ordered a hamburger and a beer, and filled out a dollar eight-spot Keno ticket. I marked the numbers at random because I was afraid that if I played the same numbers every time, I would walk in one evening, look up at the board, and discover that I had just missed winning $50,000. I rarely win much—in fact, you can't win $50,000 on a dollar eight-spot ticket—but it gives me something to think about when I'm eating alone. Which is usually.

A tall, heavyset black man with a short, graying Afro and a three-day growth slid onto the stool next to me.

"What's happening?" he grunted.

"Hello, Deke. I was going to call you. I may need some help on a case."

Deke—Deacon Adams—came to Reno some thirty years ago to be a survival instructor at Stead Air Force Base. When the program ended and the base closed, Deke stayed. I'm not sure I would have—Reno isn't the most integrated city in the world—but he figured he had no place else to go. He drifted through a variety of odd jobs, finally becoming a security guard at the Mother Lode. He worked graveyard, which meant that he was still available for occasional day work.

I told him about Joan Halliday.

"Shit. Why that woman hire you?"

"I told you. Terry recommended me."

"She got all kinds of money. Why don't she hire somebody big-time?"

"She may not have all that much. Charlie lost all his, and I don't know what an ex-chorus girl and an ex-lifeguard do for a living. And I didn't ask."

He thought about that while he studied the menu through red-rimmed eyes too small for his pear-shaped face. Former survival instructors, like former football players, end up covered with hard fat. The menu hadn't changed from the day before—or the year before—and he tossed it aside.

"So what do you need?"

"I need you to come with me when I find the car. If anybody gets upset when I start to get in it and drive away, I want you to calm them down."

"Call me," he grunted.

Diane arrived with my hamburger and took Deke's order for a steak. Casino food is so predictable it's soothing. I'd say it's like what mother used to make, but my mother didn't like to cook, and casino food is actually better.

Deke and I small-talked over a couple of beers. I played a couple more Keno tickets and—surprisingly—paid for my dinner. That's the frustrating thing about Keno. Even hitting enough to pay for dinner is a surprise. A Keno ticket has eighty numbers, and twenty of them are drawn for each game and displayed on the electronic boards all over the building. When you play eight numbers, you have to hit four just to get your dollar back. I used to start getting excited when I hit even three, but now it takes at least five. Five numbers pays five dollars, which is what I got, and actually it didn't quite pay for my dinner. Six pays about one hundred, seven about fifteen hundred, but all eight pays a big eighteen grand. It's as if a small-scale state lottery ran every fifteen minutes. Thinking about it, I didn't pay for dinner at all. I just got back what I lost while I was eating.

It was still early when I left, so I opened another beer and watched a movie when I got home, the newest Woody Allen on video. I liked him better when he was funny. There was a time when I would have fallen asleep with the doors and windows open, but the business I'm in, and the rising crime rate, have made me a bit more cautious. I locked up and turned the air conditioner on before I went to bed.

Tracing Mary Yates the next day was a piece of cake. It turned out that the daughter was on welfare—Joan Halliday hadn't mentioned grandchildren, but there were two, both boys, ages one and a half and three. I got a current address that turned out to be a shack on Sutro Street and called a university student who is willing to work for considerably less than I am and asked him to start hanging out there. I didn't worry about a twenty-four-hour stakeout, because I didn't think her mother would visit in the middle of the night. I had a couple of other things going that I had to devote some time to, but I drove by to spell the kid when I had nothing better to do.

The white Oldsmobile showed up three days later, about two in the afternoon. The student had been parking his beige Chevy van up and down that block and the ones on either side, occasionally moving just around the corner, but where he could still see the space in front of the house. He drove the few blocks to Wells Avenue and called me from a drugstore. The Olds was still there when I arrived.

About an hour later, a black woman of indeterminate age in jeans and a pink cotton blouse came out of the shack, got into the car, and drove off. I followed her back to Wells, down to Quincy, and out to a section of town that almost made me wish I were armed. I rarely carry a gun. I learned to shoot a rifle when I was nine, knocking lizards off the back fence, but I don't really like small guns. Most of the time they cause more problems than they solve. Nevertheless, there was no way I was coming back here without Deke or a gun or maybe both.

The woman turned into the driveway of a two-story frame house that appeared to have last been painted gray. It was hard to tell from the remaining flakes. I made a note of the number and, mindful of the need to check for assets, drove downtown to check out the ownership of the property.

The house was owned by Castle Properties, a privately held corporation with a Carson City post office box for an address. Dead end.

The kid agreed to watch the house the next morning to see if anybody left for a job. Nobody did.

I called Deke and told him I'd pick him up around nine.

I didn't want to take the car until everybody was settled in for the night.

It turned out that we were early. The white Oldsmobile was pulling out of the driveway just as we got there.

I drive a green '68 Ford Mustang that looks deceptively battered—it's really just dirty. I've had the engine rebuilt twice, and I knew it could go any place the Olds could. And more. I followed at a discreet distance.

"Whyn't we just wait till they come back? Or come another night?" Deke grumbled.

"Because we might learn something. Assets, remember?"

We followed the Olds out to McCarran Road and turned north. We were in the country almost immediately, passing fields where in daylight we could have seen cows grazing. I slowed down. There weren't too many places to turn off, and a full moon lit the white car like a snowbank. Just past the road to Hidden Valley, a panel truck was parked. The Olds pulled up next to it.

I drove past them about a half mile, killed the lights, and turned around. When we could just see the glimmer of white, I stopped, leaving the engine running. Someone was just slamming the Olds's trunk. A few seconds later the panel truck left, then the Olds. Both were headed away from us. I eased after them, turning on the lights as we headed right again on Quincy.

By the time we reached the house, the Olds was sitting in the driveway. I parked half a block down, waiting for the house to go dark.

"Which car do you want to drive?" I asked.

"You really want to do this? After what we saw, we could get the Man to do it for us."

"I really want to do this. We see what's in the trunk before we do anything else."

Deke squinted at me through bleary eyes.

"I hope they go to bed before midnight. I gotta be at work by one."

The downstairs lights went out about eleven, and the upstairs lights about five past twelve. I gave them another ten minutes, even though Deke was getting restless. I had the set of keys to the Olds and the paper authorizing me to drive it to Lois Barrington Hellman's residence in the pocket of my jacket, so I turned the Mustang over to Deke, padded down the block to the Olds, opened and shut the door as quietly as I could, released the brake, and let the car roll out of the driveway before I started the engine.

Nobody shouted after me. Either they were already asleep or they just didn't recognize the sound of the car.

I figured I had better check the contents of the trunk before depositing the car with Lois Barrington Hellman, who might not appreciate my barging in at that hour in any case, so I drove the Olds into my own garage. Deke parked the Mustang in front.

Inside the trunk was a plastic bag containing enough white powder to keep a Hollywood movie crew happy for a month.

"I guess we know what their assets are."

"What you gonna do now?"

"Turn it over to the Man. And I am certainly glad he's only six blocks away. Do you want me to keep you out of it?"

"How you gonna do that? Say you followed them on foot?"

"I guess not. But you could probably go to work and let them get in touch with you when they get around to it."

"I'll do that. But lemme see you safely to the door first."

"Okay. Thanks." I wanted to hug him, but he would have considered it a breach of our professional relationship.

I drove the Olds straight into the police station parking lot. Deke was leaning on the fender of the Mustang, parked at the curb, as I walked around to the front steps. He tossed me the keys.

"Take care, girl."

"Yeah. Thanks again."

I was inside the doors before he moved.

The officer at the desk—Danny Sinclair—was a burly fellow with prematurely thinning red hair and freckles that ran together on his face. We hadn't liked each other much in high school, so I wasn't surprised when he didn't like my story a whole lot. He said something about cheating welfare queens and their slimeball boyfriends poisoning the youth of our city, using words that made me wonder again why Deke or anybody else stayed here, but he called somebody from the back to cover the desk while he came out to check the car.

"Jesus," he said when he saw the contents of the package. "We're going to have to impound the car. The Barringtons may not be happy about that."

"Yeah, well, that's life. I'll tell them what happened."

"You should have called us, you know."

"I had permission to drive the car, and I didn't know what was in the trunk."

"Yeah, right. But you should have called us. Remember that the next time."

I was particularly careful about locks that night.

The next morning I called Joan Halliday at the Bonanza Inn.

"Cocaine? Are you serious?"

"Yes, ma'am."

"My God." She kind of drew it out. "Charlie being taken care of by drug dealers."

She didn't say anything more, so I had to.

"It looks that way, anyway. And I'm sorry about the car."

"No, that's all right. You did the right thing. Do you think we'll get it back?"

"I don't know. It depends." I stopped, because I didn't know what it depended on. And I really didn't think they'd get it back.

"Well, you certainly did what I asked you to do."

"Yeah. I hoped you'd feel that way."

She gave me a Las Vegas address, told me to send the bill to her there.

I did.

I also checked with Danny Sinclair, who told me that the cops couldn't pick up any prints from the plastic bag, so they couldn't charge Willie Carver or Mary Yates. No telling when the bag had been put in the trunk, or by whom. Since nobody was charged with anything, Charlie Barrington would get his car back after all.

Joan Halliday paid the bill within the week.

About a month later, out of curiosity, I drove by the house on Quincy Street. It had a pickup truck in the driveway, a tricycle on the lawn, and new curtains at the windows.

I didn't think about the case again until I read in the papers that Lois Barrington Hellman had been murdered.

Chapter

2

ACTUALLY, THE NEWSPAPERS said it was an accident. Lois had taken Charlie out for lunch—he could get around okay with a walker. They had gone to the Comstock Room, on the tenth floor of the Mother Lode. Ten floors were about as tall as anything got in Reno at the time the Mother Lode was built, although the newer hotels are taller. I've never eaten there, but I'm told the food is pretty good and the view of the mountains is spectacular. If you like brown mountains. Most of the year, though, even in July, there's a dusting of snow on top. When you fly over them, they look like stale doughnuts sifted with powdered sugar.

Anyway, as Lois and Charlie were crossing Center Street to the parking lot, a car ran the light. Lois pushed Charlie back and was hit square, tossed against a light pole that snapped her neck. The car kept going.

Charlie suffered a mild concussion when his head hit the pavement.

Eyewitnesses gave varying descriptions of the car, but the police made a for-sure identification of a black Toyota that they found two days later abandoned on the corner of Virginia and McCarran. Threads from Lois's dress were caught on the dented left front fender. The car had been rented at the airport.

I found out the rest when Joan Halliday called and asked to see me.

"The police think I did it," she told me when she arrived an hour later. "The police think that I actually wanted to murder Lois, or Charlie, or Lois and Charlie both."

This time she was wearing a blue dress that draped softly. And once again she made me realize how shabby my office was. I wondered what it would have been like if I had chosen a different kind of life. But the Mick Hallidays would never have chosen me.

"Why do they think that?"

"Two of the witnesses said the person driving the car was blond, probably a woman. It happened so quickly that no one was certain."

"But why you?"

She paused, obviously wishing she didn't have to tell me all this. Her long, thin nose looked pinched and white beneath her tan.

"To say we haven't been close is an understatement. Do—did—you know Lois?"

I shrugged. "Somebody pointed her out once as Professor Hellman's wife. But we were never formally introduced."

"What was your impression of her?"

"Overweight. Plain. Cheap clothes, cheap permanent. Even for a faculty wife, she lacked style."

I thought she might rise to her dead sister's defense, but she laughed, soundlessly.

"But we looked alike, Lois and I. When we were children. She was only two years older, and people even thought we were twins. We were close—almost as close as twins—until Charlie left Mama for that silly starlet. Then Lois decided that pretty women were bad women. And I decided looks were all you could count on to get and keep what you wanted."

"So Lois got fat and went to college and you became a dancer?"

"Yes. And she hated me for it. And she hated me for every good thing that happened to me for the next twenty-five years."

"Including Mick?"

"Especially Mick."

"Why? She was married, too."

"Yes. Poor Bob. He spent his life in Charlie's shadow, with Lois forever reminding him of all the things he wasn't. And Bob wasn't Charlie—Bob wasn't a demanding, mean, self-centered gambler. He was a kind, rather boring, ambitionless man, content to teach at a third-rate university, who for some unexplainable reason actually loved her."

"You don't like your father very much."

"I adore my father."

"Oh. So why was Lois jealous about Mick?"

"Because he was handsome, exciting, and he laughed at Charlie. He saw Charlie as one more craps dealer who got lucky, that's all. No mystique."

"Not even when the university honored Charlie as a Distinguished Nevadan? That's a long climb for a lucky craps dealer."

"Not really. He gave them a building. And then at the reception, Mick got more attention than Charlie—all the little coeds that Mick taught to swim showed up."

I turned away, not wanting to remind her that I had been one of them. Although no one had ever called me little.

"So you and Lois had a history of problems. Why would you kill her?"

"Well, I wouldn't, of course. But I was angry. About the drugs in the trunk of the car, and the trashed house. About Charlie being left to sit in his own urine while the people who were being paid to take care of him did whatever it was they were doing. About the way she ignored the problem and I had to clean it up. We went out for dinner, the two of us. I thought I could discuss it with her. But she blew up, blamed me, said it had all happened because I had left her with the responsibility and she had done the best she could, that I couldn't come back at her now. I did, though. I started yelling that if she couldn't take care of him, she should have called me, she should have let me know. Charlie is a selfish son of a bitch, but he's still my father. We were both on our feet yelling when I threw a drink at her and walked out of the restaurant.''

"Did anyone remember what you yelled at her?''

"Yes. The waitress and the busboy.''

"And what did they remember?''

"I was yelling something to the effect that I knew she was drinking herself to death, but it was taking too long. Somebody ought to do her the favor of speeding it up.''

"Then what?''

"Then I flew back to Las Vegas, and I stayed there until the police called to tell me about Lois. They didn't tell me I was a suspect, so I came back to be with Charlie. I thought he might need me.''

"He didn't?''

"Not much." She almost smiled. "Although he was concerned that he had almost died. And concerned that whoever it was may try again.''

"Didn't he care about Lois?''

"Well, he cared about what would happen now that Lois wasn't around to answer his mail, and to write his checks, and to make sure the nurses look after him, but I don't think he feels much sense of loss beyond that.''

"Does Charlie care about you?''

"As much as he cares about anyone. He still hopes I'll be buried with him.''

"O-kay." I took a deep breath, thinking about where to go next.

"I'm sorry, Freddie. I hope you aren't expecting to like any of us. We aren't a very likable family.''

But I did like her. If she had been a little less beautiful and hadn't married Mick Halliday, I might even have felt sorry for her.

"Is there any possibility that the hit-and-run was an accident?''

"Witnesses didn't think so.''

"What about Charlie?''

"He thinks it was probably some old enemy who wanted him dead. But he can't come up with anything solid enough for the police to investigate."

"You know that I can't interfere with the police investigation of a murder."

"The police aren't investigating. They think I did it. Van Woodruff is acting as my attorney, until I see how serious this really is. If it's really bad, I may need outside help. If it isn't, I'm better off with someone local. And I don't think anyone will mind if you ask a few questions."

"What about Charlie?"

"You might want to start with him. He could be right, you know. The murderer could have been after him."

"I will. Charlie and the rented car—do you know what the police found out about the rented car?"

"No. But I know I didn't rent it."

"Did you have an alibi for the time it was rented? Didn't someone know you were in Las Vegas?"

"No. I was upset about everything that had happened, Charlie and Lois and the drugs, so I drove out to Lake Mead. We have a houseboat, at Echo Bay. I was alone out there for two days."

"Somebody must have seen you—somebody else must have been on a houseboat or at the grocery store. Lake Mead is a busy place this time of year."

"I took groceries from the house. There were people around, of course, but the police tell me that doesn't mean anything. No one can swear I was there the whole time—I could have left and come back, with no one knowing."

"Did you talk to anyone who might *think* you were there the whole time? Was anyone on a nearby boat?"

"Yes, but I don't know who they were. We didn't exchange names or addresses. It was just casual conversation."

"Okay. Let me know if you can think of anyone who might help establish your alibi. In the meantime, I'll need to talk to Woodruff. Does he know you've hired me?"

"No, but I'll tell him."

"Okay. I'll be in touch."

The Golden Age Board and Care Residence and Convalescent Hospital was on Oddie Boulevard, about halfway between Reno and Sparks. I could remember when Oddie Boulevard was on the outskirts of the city, just a few houses. Now it was tract homes and minimalls. Urban blight, even in Reno, one of the last strongholds of the Old West. Or so I had thought of it as a kid. Reno was probably too glitzy for the real Old West even then. Probably any time after 1950 was too late.

I drove out there the next afternoon, on one of those days that reminded me why I stayed in Reno. The air was clear, the sky blue, and the mountains were raw gemstones, topaz and sapphire. The temperature was a mild 80, and what I really wanted to do was head for those hills, and walk, and breathe. Or maybe get in a plane and fly over them. I have a pilot's license, and I'm up there on any excuse.

Instead, I turned into a small parking lot marked Visitors. Golden Age was actually two buildings, one the board and care facility for active seniors, and the other the nursing home, for old people who couldn't get up and dressed by themselves any longer. Both were low, sprawling one-story buildings, built from the same institutional beige concrete as the high school across the street. Late fifties, I'd say. No lawns, but a lot of gravel, and a couple of sad bushes next to the entrance to the hospital. That's where Charlie was, the convalescent hospital.

I pushed through the glass doors into a foyer with a couple of green armchairs and a scratched table with some tattered magazines. A cheap desert landscape, complete with purple sagebrush, decorated the walls. When I reached the nurse's station, I was hit with the smell, urine overlaid with ammonia, that always frightens me in hospitals. The smell of helplessness.

I knew the nurse—Mrs. Schueller, Kristin Schueller's mother. That tells you how small Reno still is, underneath all the new glitz. Nobody who grew up here can go anywhere without running into somebody who remembers her in diapers. Kristin and I had been in Girl Scouts together, and I had felt sorry for her because her mother had to work. That was right before my father left for Nam and Mom got a job with the phone company. She kept the job when he got back.

Mrs. Schueller remembered me, and when I asked politely about Kristin told me that Kristin had graduated from law school, married a classmate, moved to Los Angeles, and had a two-year-old son. She didn't even spare me the baby pictures. I wouldn't like baby pictures even if they were my own. In fact, feeling as I do about babies, my own would even have been worse. It was ten minutes before she put them away and gave me directions to Charlie's room— down the hall to the right, through the social room, a left, another left, then third door on the right.

The social room was an open space with a few tables, a big corkboard covered with flyers, and a small group of fuzzy white-haired women in wheelchairs staring out the windows. I hurried down the hall.

Charlie's door was open. He was lying on his bed, fully dressed, watching television. The room had evidently been a double at one time, because there was one of those shower-curtain type arrangements for screening off the area where the other bed would have been. Even without a second bed, there wasn't a lot of room. Charlie's bed was close to the window—actually a sliding door leading to a small cement patio. There was nothing but a chair on the patio, and nothing to see but a wall. The television set was perched on top of a dresser at the foot of the bed. A hospital table that slides over the top of the bed was pushed to one side. One large, green, overstuffed armchair, a relative of the ones in the foyer, sat defiantly in the space where there wasn't a second bed. There were a lot of greeting cards taped to the walls. That was it.

Charlie ignored my first knock, so I tried again, louder.

He looked up slowly, then raised his eyebrows above the blue glasses that had always been his trademark.

"I thought you was a nurse," he growled. "Come on in."

Charlie had always been tall and lean, but age and illness had made him stooped and gaunt. The long-sleeved, light blue, western-style shirt was too big for the thin frame, the bony wrists. Instead of a tie, a black cord was held close to his throat by a hunk of turquoise and silver. His buckle matched, and so did a ring on his right hand. He should have been wearing boots, but he wasn't. Slippers.

I introduced myself, trying to see past those glasses to his eyes. I couldn't. The glasses perched on a sharp nose that jutted over a sunken chin. He still had a full head of white hair, although it was starting to thin. His old-man skin was dry, wrinkling, spotted. I shook his spotted hand. The turquoise stone had a crack across one corner.

"Freddie O'Neal? Did I know your father?"

"I don't think so, sir."

He waved me toward the chair, and I sat.

"What can I do for you?"

A colorized Humphrey Bogart disappeared from the television screen with a flick of the remote control.

I told him his daughter had hired me, and he chuckled.

"Joan told me she hired a private eye. I didn't expect a girl. Kinda tall for a girl, ain'tcha?"

There was no point challenging him, so I didn't.

I murmured something like "Guess so, sir," and waited for him to go on, but he didn't. We sat there in silence until I said, "Would you mind telling me what happened?"

"No, I don't mind. Some damn fool tried to kill me and got Lois instead. Then some other damn fool figured Joan did it and arrested her. I been telling the cops that, but they think I'm an old fool trying to protect my daughter. Hell, I wouldn't try to protect her. If I thought she'd tried to kill me, I'd say so."

"I believe you. What happened the day of the accident?"

"Didn't see a thing. Had a tasty lunch in the Comstock Room—a steak sandwich on sourdough bread, and fried potatoes, and some tomato slices, and coffee. It was a real steak, a real lunch. I don't get out much, you know, and the food here stinks. I'm losing weight because there's nothing to eat here. I wanted Lois to move me, but she wouldn't do it. She said I had to stay here. She said there wasn't enough money for anywhere else. So we finished lunch and left the club. I used to own that club, and they won't let me pay for anything. Anytime I come in, I get a free lunch. But Lois never liked to take me out. She'd get impatient, because I walk so slow, with the walker. Joan takes me, when she's in town, she doesn't mind, and she likes to get the free lunch, but she isn't here much. I started to cross the street, and I don't remember what happened next. I got my head busted pretty bad, though. Here, feel this."

He reached for my hand, and I had to get up and move closer to the bed. He rubbed my hand across the back of his head, where there was indeed a knot.

"Who might have wanted to kill you?"

"Oh, hell, I don't know. Maybe lots of people. This used to be a pretty rough town, you know. Maybe somebody wanted to settle a score from the old days."

"Who? What kind of a score?"

His mouth worked, but he didn't say anything. I was really annoyed at his apparent lack of concern for Lois. I sat back down and waited.

"Maybe somebody thinks I owe'm something," he said finally.

"Charlie, that doesn't help. I have to have something more than that."

"Well, there's Julie. She might have wanted to kill me."

"Your first wife? She might have wanted to kill you, but I can't imagine that she'd kill Lois and let Joan take the rap. Of course, I don't know her," I added hastily as he glared at me. Even through the blue glasses, I knew he was glaring.

"Well, maybe not. But there were some guys in the

movie business—I lost a lot of money making movies, you know. Maybe somebody was still mad at me.''

''Who?''

''Or maybe somebody thinks I have something I don't have, or that they get something when I die.''

He tapped the bed restlessly and stared out the window at the patio wall.

''Charlie—did you know that the woman who was taking care of you—what was her name—did you know that she and her boyfriend were dealing drugs out of your house?''

''No, Lois said that, and I don't believe it. Mary wouldn't do that. But maybe somebody thinks so.''

I couldn't tell whether he was lying or not. He plucked at the bedspread.

''Is there anything you can tell me that might help? Are there any names you can think of?''

''No. But probably a lot I can't think of.''

He picked up the remote control and turned the television back on. A colorized Lauren Bacall was just saying, ''You know how to whistle, don't you?''

''You want to stay and watch this movie with me?'' Charlie asked. ''It's a good one. I don't remember how it ends, though. And after the movie, it's time for *Hour of Power*. You ever watch *Hour of Power?*''

''No, and today isn't a good time to start. I think I'd better get going. Your daughter's paying me to find out who tried to kill you, and I work by the hour.''

His face sagged, and I felt as if it had been a cheap shot.

''I'm sorry about Lois,'' he said. ''I didn't want her to die. It's just I can't do nothing about it, so I don't think about it much. I hope you find who did it. Come back if you have any more questions.''

I started to thank him, but he was already absorbed in the rainbow screen. I retraced my steps to the front door, waved at Mrs. Schueller, and left.

Twenty cents in a pay phone elicited the information that Van Woodruff was still out of the office. For twenty-four hours he had been out of the office. I decided to show up and see what happened.

Woodruff's office was on the third floor of the First Nevada National Bank building. Since I didn't know how long I was going to have to wait, I drove my car home and left it there. The afternoon was pleasant, the walk was a little more than a mile, and it was easier than worrying about parking.

Woodruff, Wallace, Manoukian and Lagomarsino occupied the entire third floor of the building. The reception area was teak and beige, reeking of expensive taste. The young woman behind the large desk was Jackie Urrutia, the youngest of the six Urrutia girls. Kenny Urrutia—the only boy in the family—had been a big high-school football star. He sat behind me in geometry, and I let him copy my papers, violating my sense of integrity because I hoped he would ask me out sometime. He didn't.

I handed Jackie my card and asked about Van Woodruff.

"Mr. Woodruff isn't in," she said. She had to toss her long, straight black hair out of her face in order to look up at me. One lock got caught in her earrings, which dangled almost to her shoulders, so she left it. Who says the sixties aren't coming back. "He's in court, he has been all week. Usually he comes in for a few minutes at the end of the day, but only for urgent business. Then he has to get to rehearsal."

Van Woodruff was the Reno Theatrical Society's answer to Cary Grant. He always starred in at least one play per season, usually a romantic comedy or a romantic mystery. I thought about going to the theater and trying to talk with him during a break, but I knew that would annoy him. I sat down to wait instead.

I had read three back issues of *Time* from cover to cover, knowing more about June than anyone else knows by September, when Van Woodruff walked in. He really was sort of Cary Grantish. About six feet three, elegantly slender, three-piece Italian suit. Wings of gray hair swept back from his temples. Black-rimmed glasses over piercing dark eyes. Even a dimple in his chin.

Joan Halliday had indeed called him, and he agreed to see me for a moment. I followed him around the receptionist and down the hall to a large teak and beige private office. There was an abstract brass sculpture on the wall that on closer inspection turned out to be a clock. Woodruff dropped his briefcase on his desk with a force that startled me.

I've learned to have a no-nonsense attitude toward handsome men. In Woodruff's case, it was easy. He didn't care if he charmed me.

"I appreciate your concern for Mrs. Halliday," he told me, not smiling, not sitting, not offering me a seat. We stood there, almost eye to eye. "But I don't think there's anything you can do to help her. The signature on the car rental agreement is hers. The district attorney and I are working on a plea bargain, temporary insanity, no jail time."

"You're kidding."

His raised eyebrows were supposed to show that he wasn't.

"What about the clerk who rented the car? Could she identify Mrs. Halliday?" I asked.

"Not positively. But she couldn't say it wasn't Mrs. Halliday, either."

"Fingerprints on the car?"

"None."

"Any other evidence?"

"No."

"You want her to plead guilty on such a weak case?"

He looked at me as if he had better things to do.

"Not guilty. Not guilty by reason of temporary insanity. Two people heard the threat, her signature is on the car rental, and she has no alibi. Nobody wants this case to go to trial. We all remember Charlie too well to want one of his daughters to go to jail for killing the other. This is the best solution for all concerned."

His phone started ringing, and I was obviously dismissed.

By the time I reached home, I had almost managed to walk off the head of steam I had built up in Woodruff's office. I tried to call Joan Halliday to tell her to get a new lawyer, but there was no answer. My next stop was the airport, which was too far to walk.

I didn't know the small, harried young woman at the rent-a-car counter. Probably a divorcee who came to Reno for a new start, couldn't find it, and realized she had nothing to go back to.

"That was Lurene," she said. "Lurene handled it. The police already talked to her."

Wisps of brown hair hung over her face, and she didn't bother to brush them back. It was a rabbity face, small nose that looked like it ran a lot. Maybe she cried at night.

"When will Lurene be back?"

"Not till tomorrow morning. She's on days now—she's rehearsing a play at the Reno Theatrical Society at night. Some kind of comedy."

I thought again about crashing the rehearsal, but I still didn't think I'd gain anything.

"Thanks. I'll try to catch her tomorrow."

As I turned off Mill Street toward home, I saw a red Corvette parked in front of my house. I don't travel in red Corvette circles. But I remembered the man sitting on my porch.

Mick Halliday. And he was smiling.

Chapter 3

BLUSHING IS DUMB, of course, and a blushing person never projects an image of authority, never looks in control of the situation, and who would ever hire a blushing PI? But when Mick stood up, all muscular five feet ten inches of him, with his curly black hair and bright blue eyes and John F. Kennedy smile unchanged after all these years, and held out his arms to me, I couldn't help remembering the first time I met him.

I was a pudgy eight-year-old suffering from what seemed to be an unconquerable fear of the water, stemming from the time two years earlier when my fifteen-year-old cousin had thrown me into a pool and then jumped in after me and held my head under until I thought I was going to drown. He let me up for air and then held me under again, just for the fun of feeling me struggle. I was determined that I wasn't going to let that happen again, so I stayed away from both water and my cousin. My mother—who didn't know the root of my fear, since I never ratted—thought I really ought to learn to swim, and signed me up for lessons when it became obvious that I would never do it on my own.

That first Saturday morning I got as far as the top step in the shallow end and refused to go any farther, while younger and braver kids plunged in on both sides. Mick came over to see why I was just standing there.

"I'm scared," I told him, shivering to emphasize my point.

"Come on," he said. "It's okay—I'll catch you."

He was standing about two feet from the bottom of the steps, arms outstretched. The distance seemed infinite.

"Come on," he said again. And he smiled at me, a smile that seemed to promise that all I had to do was reach out and he would not only catch me, he would hold me and love me forever.

I jumped. And he caught me. When my mother arrived at the end of the lesson, I showed her how I could do the dead man's float. That was one of the rare occasions my mother was caught speechless. By the end of the summer, I was practically a performing porpoise. I cried when I had to leave Mick. I saw him occasionally as long as he was at the Sierra Madre, and I had matured sufficiently by the time he married that all I felt was a tiny pang of the old crush.

Now, twenty-or-so years later, Mick Halliday was standing there smiling and holding his arms out. Maybe he was a little bulkier than he used to be—the open sports jacket exposed the beginning of a belly. Maybe there were a few lines around the eyes, and the skin showing on his neck and collarbone above the green polo shirt was a little mottled, as if maybe he drank a bit, but the smile was as compelling as ever, still seeming to promise eternal love. So I blushed. I took his right hand and shook it.

"Freddie, you look great," he said, winking a baby blue. "I knew you'd be gorgeous when you grew up."

"Thanks, Mick." I accept compliments even when I don't believe them. I have strong features, and one might say that I look intelligent, or that I have character, but I don't wear makeup, and even if I did, I still wouldn't be gorgeous. "You were gorgeous then and you haven't changed at all. Come on in."

He followed me into my office and sat in one of the folding chairs when I gestured. I really would have to do something about the office. He turned down my offer of a beer.

"Just here for a minute—alas. I wish I'd planned to stay longer. Next time. It'll be social, not business, and I'll bring the beer."

"Sure, Mick."

I sat down behind my desk and waited.

"About Joan hiring you—Freddie, it's no good going on with this."

"What do you mean? You think she did it?"

"Who else?"

"Well, that's the point, isn't it? That's why she hired me."

"Freddie, she hired you as a cover, to make it look as if she's innocent. Of course she killed Lois. It'll be okay, really it will. Woodruff will plead temporary insanity, and she won't do a day for it. Now, how much do you want to cover your time—plus a little for expenses, of course?"

He pulled out his checkbook, still smiling.

"Even if she killed Lois, why would she have risked Charlie like that?"

"Charlie? Charlie's already dead, has been for years. It's only a matter of time until his heart stops and makes it official. What difference does Charlie make?"

"Well, he may be a selfish son of a bitch, but he is her father. And nobody heard her make threats against him."

"And he wasn't hurt."

He still had pen and checkbook in hand, but the smile was a little strained. This time, I wasn't jumping in.

"I can't, Mick. Your wife is my client, and I can't sell her out. She can call me if she decides to accept the plea bargain, and I'll send her a bill."

"You're a woman of principle, Freddie, and I admire that. I'll tell Joan you stood up for her, against the evidence."

He put the checkbook and pen back in the pocket of his jacket.

"Thanks."

The smile brightened again as he said good-bye.

I thought about telling Joan Halliday she didn't just need

a new lawyer, she needed a new husband, too. Whether she knew it or not, she was swimming alone.

When she hadn't called me by ten o'clock the next morning, I decided I was still on the case. I called Las Vegas on my modem and left a message on Rudy Stapp's computer, asking him to nose around Echo Bay, see if anyone might have seen Joan Halliday at Lake Mead. Hiring Rudy was cheaper, and I hoped faster, than flying down and doing it myself. Then I drove back to the airport to see Lurene.

Lurene looked as if she were working rent-a-car because she hadn't quite made the cut for casino change girl. Or maybe the coins and the changer were just too heavy for her. She was model-frail and almost pretty—permed blond hair framing a heart-shaped face that probably looked better with stage makeup. Another seeker after a glamorous restart who hadn't made it past the airport. Which was too bad. If she'd been a native, she might have remembered Joan Halliday. Or *not* Joan Halliday.

As it was, she was blank.

"The police asked me," she said. "And I just don't know. I have no idea what the woman who signed the rental agreement looked like."

"Blond? Not blond? Young? Old? Nothing?"

"Nothing. Really. Why would I remember somebody?"

Why indeed? Why would Joan Halliday have drawn attention to herself if she were renting a car to murder her sister? Why would anyone forging Joan Halliday's name to a rental form have drawn attention to herself? Why had I expected anything else?

I left the airport, picked up 395 North, zipped to Interstate 80, and turned north on Virginia Street. Reno still seemed too small to me to need freeways, but I guess they came with the biggest-little-city territory. And they certainly made it easy to get from the airport to the university.

I've always liked the campus, probably because I spent a couple of good years there. A couple of them weren't so good, but that, of course, is life. The campus looked pretty ordinary, brick buildings and trees and lots of open, grassy spaces filled with lounging students. But it was really peculiarly Nevadan. The quad, which was off to one side of the campus, featured a statue of John Mackay, discoverer of the Comstock Lode. Mackay crossed the Sierras from California to Nevada—as did many forty-niners who failed to strike gold—with a partner.

Legend has it that as they reached the state line, Mackay said to his partner, "I'm broke. How much have you got?" The answer was "Fifty cents." Mackay allegedly said, "Throw it away. Let's start fresh." The partner was never heard from again, another name lost in history. Would Mackay have thrown away the fifty cents if it had been his? Did he perhaps go back and pick it up? In any case, he found silver. And funded the Mackay School of Mines. That's where the quad and the statue were, in front of the Mackay School of Mines. Engineering and nursing were on that side of the campus, too.

I almost never saw those buildings in four years. That entire section of the campus was alien to me. The humanities, where I put in my time, were housed in an old brick building with AGRICVLTVRE carved in concrete over the front door. Just in case anyone forgot what land-grant universities were all about. I have no idea where the new agriculture building was. There was a story that two philosophy professors had planned to fill in the AGRI one night, but it never happened.

And lest it be said the Nevadans have misplaced values, the university had a beautiful new Fine Arts complex. Several Distinguished Nevadan Awards were doubtless involved in the funding. I don't know that for sure, but nobody in Reno did anything for free.

Professor Hellman's office was in the basement of the AGRICVLTVRE building. He had had that same office for about fifteen years, since he quit being chair of the department, but the bookshelves looked as if they had been accumulating treasures and dust since the Fall of the Roman Empire. The shelves filled every square foot of wall space from the floor to the low ceiling, except for the high rectangular window on the wall behind the desk. The window afforded a glorious view of dirt, grass, and feet. More books and a number of journals were stacked on a table, which also held the overflow of treasures, an eclectic collection that included arrowheads and a tomahawk next to a replica of a statue of Hercules. A framed reproduction of Danae awaiting the Shower of Gold hung from a divider between two bookcases.

At first I didn't think Professor Hellman was there. He was almost completely hidden from view behind a desk in a high-backed leather chair that was turned toward the wall. We were equally startled when the chair turned and he appeared. He hadn't heard me come in.

"You may not remember me—" I started gamely, but he interrupted.

"Of course I do, Freddie. You wrote a very interesting paper on the classical images of women warriors, focusing particularly on the Goddess Athena, Penthesilea and the Amazons, and Camilla from the *Aeneid*. About ten years ago, I think."

"Thank you. Yes, it was about that long ago."

Hellman looked like a professor. He looked soft, as if he didn't exercise, and his body had a definite slope. The heavy gray cardigan sweater he was wearing over a green plaid shirt even had leather patches at the elbows. Long wisps of gray hair sprang from the top of his head. His pale brown eyes, large behind thick, black-rimmed glasses, seemed focused somewhere beyond me. I remembered him as one of those professors who drove you nuts as they read their lectures, until you shut your eyes and listened. Then you were blown away—the guy was bright. But I still hadn't expected him to remember the paper.

"Thinking of coming back for a master's degree? We'd love to have you."

"Thanks, but no, no, I wasn't thinking of that. That's not why I'm here."

"What can I do for you then?"

Shit. She hadn't told him.

"Your sister-in-law, Joan Halliday, has hired me. I'm a private investigator. She wants me to find out who might have killed your wife, and I'm sorry, Professor Hellman, I really am."

I was searching for more words when he held up his hand to stop me.

"No, it's all right, Freddie. Joan should have told me, but it's all right." He paused, blinking his soft eyes. "Please sit down."

I moved a stack of papers from the chair in front of the desk, placing them on top of another stack already on the table.

"Only September, and they're already piling up," he said sadly.

"Yes," I said, settling uncomfortably in the chair. "Professor Hellman, I'd appreciate it if you would tell me as much as you can. About your wife, her relationship with her sister, about anybody who might have wanted to hurt her, about what you think happened that day."

"Well, probably what you want to know first of all is whether I think Joan killed Lois. And the answer is, I don't think so. In fact, I'm glad she hired someone to help her, since it appears the police think she's guilty."

"Why do you think she's innocent?"

"Why are you surprised?"

"Well—it's just—"

"That no one else thinks so, except for Charlie. I know. But I've known Joan for a number of years now, and I simply don't think she's capable of plotting to kill Lois in cold blood. Not that they got along—they didn't. Everyone gave up the idea of family holidays long ago. I'm afraid my wife had a tendency to drink too much, and she would then accuse her sister of numerous crimes, both real and imagined. The worst of which was probably that she led her own life, without reference to Charlie. And Joan would put up with it as long as she could, and then she would start yelling. Certainly, Joan could be volatile and impulsive. But not murderous. Joan walks away from fights, she doesn't seek them out.''

"Then who do you think killed her—and why put it on Mrs. Halliday?''

"Well, of course, Joan is vulnerable. I'm sure she threatened Lois in the restaurant, just as the witnesses said. But as to who would do that—frame her, as it were—I have no idea. Nor do I have any idea who would want to kill Lois.''

"Did Mrs. Hellman say anything out of the ordinary, was there anything she was upset about when she went to meet her father?''

"No, not that I remember. She always complained about how onerous it was, taking Charlie out to lunch, but whenever Joan offered to move him to Las Vegas, she simply wouldn't hear of it. And I think the complaints that day were the usual ones.''

"Which were?''

"Well, that Charlie never asked what she was doing, never cared about her life, only wanted to talk about himself. That sort of thing.''

"Okay.'' I thought for a moment. "What about Charlie? He seems to think someone might have been trying to kill him, not Lois. Do you think that's possible?''

"Well, of course it's possible. He said something about that at the funeral. In fact, he apologized to me. For the first time since I've known him.'' Professor Hellman brightened at the thought. "He said 'they' wanted him, and he was sorry 'they' got Lois instead.''

"Did he tell you who 'they' are?''

"No. And considering it's Charlie, there could be a lot of 'theys' or no 'theys' whatsoever. He has always been quite a storyteller, and he is always the protagonist of his stories. I hesitate to use the word 'hero.' His stories are probably at least partly true, but as a historian, I know that truth is often a matter of interpretation and perspective. Have you talked to him about it?''

"Yes, but I'm not sure it helped. Can you think of anything else that I ought to know?"

"No. But is there some way I can get in touch with you, should anything occur to me?"

"Sure." I gave him my card. "Thanks."

He looked at my card.

"You really are a private investigator," he said, as if it had just registered.

"Yes, sir, I am."

"You were such a good student—quiet, but intelligent. I always wondered what became of you. Whatever made you decide to become a private investigator?"

I had to think before I answered, whether to just put him off. But I decided he really wanted to know.

"I took a psychology course as part of my general ed requirement, when I was still trying to figure out what I wanted to major in, and I couldn't even imagine what came next after college. One of the things the professor said was that no matter how well suited people are for a job, they aren't happy doing it unless it fits their self-image. And I realized I didn't have any kind of clear self-image. So I signed up for a career counseling test, one that asks you about yourself, about what you like to do and when you're happy. It told me I had a strong sense of right and wrong, liked to solve puzzles, needed meaningful work, and couldn't take orders. There were several career possibilities associated with the profile, but the one that stuck with me was private investigator."

"Really? I wasn't aware that anybody ever made an important decision because of one of those tests." He stopped, embarrassed. "I'm glad to know they're useful."

"That one was for me." I held out my hand. "Thanks again for your time."

"You're welcome. Tell Joan she has my support. And let me know if you decide on that master's degree. I'm still not convinced those tests are all they're cracked up to be."

I walked up the slope from the AGRICVLTVRE building to the Student Union to get coffee and a sandwich, thinking about what Professor Hellman had said. About the Barringtons, not the graduate degree. Even if Charlie was a self-centered blowhard, it made more sense that someone was trying to kill him and hit Lois by mistake. Was Charlie still in danger then? And who would—who could—forge Joan's signature?

Neither coffee nor sandwiches had improved in ten years. The students had gotten younger, but everybody says that. It's still true.

I drove down Sierra Street, past the Reno Theatrical Society, and noted the display poster advertising the next play, a farce about a British vicar married to an American actress. I imagined, with some difficulty, Van Woodruff as a British vicar. Lurene was probably playing the maid. I took California to Arlington, then out Skyline Boulevard. The scenery—and the houses—improved as I drove. The southwest section of Reno was where the Money lived. However lousy the divorce settlement had been, Julie Barrington must have gotten something, and she had invested it well. I was into horse country by the time I found her address. The house was white, ranch style, and half an acre back from the road. There were two cars in the driveway, a new Chevy Blazer and an aging Mercury Cougar.

I had to ring the bell twice before someone came to the door. The woman who opened it had the most amazing white hair I've ever seen—flowing, uncombed, to her shoulders, falling over her face, which was free of makeup and almost unlined. Her eyes were a clear brown, the only part of her that reminded me of Joan Halliday. She was wearing an ankle-length caftan of unbleached cotton. Her feet were bare. The twisted toes betrayed her age more surely than her face or even her hair.

"What?" she asked.

I introduced myself.

She shrugged.

"Come on in. I gotta keep working, I hope you don't mind."

She turned without waiting for a reply. I followed her down a hall to the back of the house, a room with a wall of windows and a bright northern exposure. Her studio. Canvases in various stages of completion leaned against otherwise bare walls. Some were landscapes, the hills as seen through the windows. Others were studies of a very naked young man, as was the canvas currently on the easel. The same very naked young man was sitting on a brass daybed, smoking a cigarette.

"Break's over," Julie Barrington snapped, taking a puff from a cigarette that had been smoldering in a large but overflowing ashtray next to the easel.

The young man stubbed out his cigarette, leaned back against a mound of pillows covered with blue cabbage roses, and resumed the Duchess of Alba pose that had been roughly sketched onto the canvas. Julie Barrington picked up a paintbrush as she studied him. She had evidently decided to skip the introductions. Or maybe she had forgotten I was there.

I didn't know where to look. So I looked at the paintings. I don't know much about art beyond a single required Art Appreciation course, so I don't know how good she was. But her work had life, vibrancy, and she paid attention to detail. Every muscle was carefully rounded, every curl of pubic hair glistened in the painted sunlight. The man was in his twenties, dark, tousled hair curling around an almost pretty face, with a slender, wiry body. I tried to imagine what he looked like with clothes on. Finally, I sat on the floor, facing Julie Barrington, my back to the daybed.

"Mrs. Barrington, I'm sorry to intrude—" I stopped. I certainly wasn't intruding on her grief.

"Yes, I know. Call me Julie—I haven't been Mrs. Barrington for years."

"Okay, Julie." Actually, it would have been easier to intrude on her grief. I didn't know how to intrude on her indifference. So I tried the rough approach. "Do you have any idea who might have wanted to kill your daughter?"

"Oh, for heaven's sake, nobody wanted to kill Lois. Nobody would have cared enough to kill Lois. And certainly not Joan. If Joan had been killed, that would have been a different story. I could imagine someone wanting to kill Joan. Lois killing Joan, that I might have believed. But not the other way round. Somebody tried to kill Charlie, it has to be that. They got Lois by mistake."

"Who? Why?"

"Isn't that what Joan's paying you to find out? I haven't been around any of 'em for years. And none of them ever came to see me."

"Excuse me, Julie, may I say something?" The model's voice was nasal, unexpectedly high.

"Sure, but don't move your body."

"The rumor around the club is drugs."

"Around the club?" I turned and stared at his face, directly into his eyes. They were pale blue and vacant, spoiling the prettiness of his face.

"I work swing shift at the Mother Lode, dealing craps. There's a rumor Charlie had something to do with drugs."

"What else does the rumor say?"

He shrugged. Julie paused to glare.

"Nothing."

"Who told you the rumor?"

"I don't know—I think two or three people. It's just one of those rumors, you know, sort of in the air, that somebody wanted to kill Charlie because of drugs."

"Thanks. I'll check on it." I sat there for another moment, but neither of them seemed to have anything more to say. "Well, I guess I'll see myself out."

Julie nodded and waved her paintbrush at me.

I thought about looking through the rest of the house—I figured nobody would stop me—but there didn't seem to be any point. I walked down the hall to the front door and left.

Joan Halliday was right. They weren't a very likable family.

Chapter

4

DEKE CHEWED HIS steak in silence, red-rimmed eyes doing his customary security-guard scan of the room. I watched the numbers light up on the Keno board. I lost.

"Maybe," Deke said, startling me.

"What? Maybe what?"

"Maybe what you asked. Maybe I know something about the rumors."

I had asked the question so much earlier that I hadn't connected it with the answer. I hadn't even really expected an answer. Although that question was the reason I had looked for Deke at the Mother Lode.

"What do you know? And why didn't you tell me when you first heard them?"

"Don't really know much, except they're around. And I didn't think nothing about them. I thought they come from the stuff we found in the trunk. Thought it was all exaggerated, people saying there was drug dealing out of Charlie's old house. And I didn't think it had nothing to do with Charlie—I thought it was the folks supposed to be taking care of him. And I still think that. That's why. Besides, there's so much dope around the casinos, why would it be special what Charlie was doing?"

"Yeah. I know. Anything you want has always been easy to get at a casino. You're probably the only employee of the Mother Lode that doesn't have a habit."

Deke shook his head.

"Nobody old as I am has one. Everybody who did is dead. Some of the kids have a habit, hasn't got to them yet. Kids your age."

"And even younger."

Every once in a while it annoys me when Deke takes it seriously that he's old enough to be my father.

"It doesn't make sense that anybody would try to kill Charlie because he was dealing drugs," I said. "Even if he had crossed somebody, this was hardly an execution-style hit. But maybe I'd better try to check it out, take a look at where Charlie used to live. And maybe I ought to give tracking down Mary Yates another try. At least talk to her, find out where she was when Mrs. Hellman was killed."

Deke grunted. "You see any trouble, you call me."

I got out a dollar and placed it on my dead Keno ticket. Both were picked up instantly by a tired woman with long, graying hair who in truth didn't care if I won or lost, but who wished me an automatic "Good luck." Keno runners used to be cheery and young. I think it's easier to lose to someone who smiles at you. At the same time, I'm glad to see middle-aged Keno runners, even if they don't smile. My backup plan, if I fail at life, is to become a Keno runner. Or a twenty-one dealer. In the sixties, women dealers had slightly racy reputations. They were, after all, paid the same salary as the men, and as my father put it, that spoiled them for other jobs. (The sixties in Reno were sort of like the fifties everywhere else. The sixties as the rest of the world knew them hit Reno about 1972.) Now, it doesn't seem like a bad job to have for a while, if you don't mind the monotony and the occasional abusive language from losing gamblers. Actually, the casinos will throw out abusive losers—it's abusive winners that you're stuck with. Being a change runner if I lose at life is out—the uniforms are brief, and even today I wouldn't look good with a bikini wax. My legs are long enough, but they're a little too muscular to be sexy.

When I lost again, I finished my beer, said good night to Deke, and rode down the escalator. I thought about picking up a movie on my way home, wondered what time it was, and wished for a moment that I had a watch. Watches are the only way to tell time in Reno. Casinos are bubbles in the world of time, with no clocks or daylight or any other way to judge what is going on outside. There are sequined lounge singers belting the blues at four in the afternoon and four in the morning. Standards from the forties and fifties, articulating the otherwise ineffable sorrow of the midafternoon torch singer. Hairstyles and makeup change, but the songs and the gowns don't.

I can't see change in Reno if I think about it from day to day, or from year to year, but sometimes I can if I think historically, from decade to decade. Tourist wear is more unisex now, with more women in jeans and jackets, fewer in dresses. The latest fashion seems to be cat sweatshirts with jeweled eyes. Most of the wonderful old slot machines with cherries and plums and lemons—the old Liberty Belles—have been replaced with less colorful bars and blanks, or the ubiquitous five-card-draw machines. Some have buttons to push, saving the weak or the lazy from even pulling a handle. And more machines urge you to play up to five coins, flashing the promise of big payoffs.

The old family-owned casinos, run by cowboy gamblers like Charlie Barrington, have mostly given way to corporations. Harold Smith and Bill Harrah are gone, and even the Harold's Club sign, the Old West mural that dominated the street all my teen years, has changed—the waterfall doesn't run anymore, and the Indians look faded amid the surrounding neon. Virginia Street seems crowded and overbuilt, and Fourth and Virginia, once the Crossroads of the World (or at least two interstates, before the freeways), is now just another corner.

I don't even want to comment on the ''new'' Reno arch. The old one was cheap and arrogant, a gambler in a black suit and a string tie named Slick, sitting at a corner table shuffling the cards and waiting for his mark. The new one is politely middle class, subdued, the con man in pinstripe who buys you a drink as he's lifting your wallet. And he's learned from the drug-dealers—he'll give you a taste of the product, knowing you'll come back for more. Five free nickels, fifty cents off on a Keno ticket, but only the first time. Then you pay.

Reno has always had a split personality—part college town, part den of sin; part Old Money escaping California taxes, part easy-come-easy-go; part nineteenth-century settlers with roots, part twentieth-century wanderers—but both Dr. Jekyll and Mr. Hyde had a certain charm. Lately, the gaudy heart of the city seems—like Mr. Hyde—to be increasingly degenerate and increasingly asserting its dominance over the more austere head. I think I liked it better when the head was in control. I feel uneasy about values, when Hansel and Gretel Children's Shoppe goes out of business and is replaced by a porn purveyor. And when drugs become so easy to get that neither Deke nor I believe that anyone would try to kill Charlie Barrington just because he was dealing cocaine. If he was dealing cocaine.

There were two messages waiting when I got home. The first was on my answering machine—Joan Halliday wanted me to call her in the morning. The second was on my modem—my buddy in Las Vegas had found somebody in Echo Bay who thought he remembered Joan Halliday on the right day. Actually, there was a third—I had forgotten to feed Butch and Sundance, and they had left quail feathers all over my office floor to warn me never to do that again. I cleaned up the feathers and other remains before I watched the movie I had picked up, a male-bonding cop movie that put me to sleep.

I tried Joan Halliday in the morning and got a machine. I sent a thank you on my machine to a Las Vegas machine. And I got Charlie Barrington's last address out of my files. Sometimes I can go for days, and my most meaningful interactions are with cats and machines. I opened a can of Purina early, to discourage foraging.

Charlie had been living with Mary Yates and her friend in a small brick house nestled among other small brick houses on Roberts Street. The neighborhood was slightly southeast of downtown, middle class sliding downward. I knocked on the door and no one answered. The yard wasn't much— already turning brown for the winter, and no flowers to care. In fact, this wasn't a good neighborhood for yards. The whole block looked tired.

I tried houses on both sides with no luck. Across the street and over one, a tall woman with short gray hair opened the door when I rang. She was wearing a flowered apron over what could only be called a housedress. I didn't think anyone wore flowered aprons anymore. Or housedresses.

"Not really," she said when I asked if she knew Charlie Barrington. "We were only neighbors for a short time, and he didn't go out of the house very much. And, of course, he moved a few months ago—I think to a nursing home—I'm not certain. Why do you want to know?"

I looked at the thin face, the sallow skin, the pale blue eyes. I told her the truth.

"Oh, my," she said, her face lighting up. "Oh, my. Well, I don't know that I can help—I really didn't know either Mrs. Hellman or Mrs. Halliday, but they both seemed like such nice people—won't you come in? Would you like coffee? It'll only take a second."

As she opened the screen door, I walked past her into the living room, declining the coffee. The room, like the woman, probably had seen better days and was surely headed for worse. The Salvation Army might think twice about accepting the furniture. Faded brown chintz covered two armchairs, a scarred metal lamp with a torn shade perched on a small table between them. I sat on a mustard bedspread that had been thrown over a small sofa. The over-the-couch art was a framed museum poster of Van Gogh's "Irises," the wrong size for the spot and I would have thought the wrong taste for the woman. She plopped into one of the armchairs, leaning forward, hands clasped on her knees. I was the most exciting thing that had happened to her in years.

I asked her to tell me everything she remembered about Charlie, about Mary, and about anyone who came to visit them.

She started with the day they moved in—the van, the furniture, how one of Mary's grandchildren ran into the street and almost got hit by a car.

"What about visitors? Did many people come to see Charlie?" I cut her off. I wanted what she knew, but not one day at a time.

"No, not really. And you'd think they would, with him having been such a big man in town. There was Mary's brother, of course—at least she said he was her brother, but some thought he wasn't—he finally moved in with them—and Stephanie and the children were there a lot, and some other colored people that must of been their friends came sometimes. Charlie's daughters—more often Mrs. Hellman, but sometimes Mrs. Halliday—and sometimes that nice son-in-law of his. No one else on any kind of regular basis—or I don't think so, but of course I don't spend my days looking out the window watching."

"Did you happen to see anything after Charlie moved—before Mary and Willie left?"

"Oh, yes. The other colored people were here a lot more then. And there were comings and goings at night, not just during the day. There was some of that while Charlie was there, but not as much. And they must of left it a terrible mess—I heard Mrs. Halliday and Mrs. Hellman arguing on the front porch, and then Mrs. Halliday was here a lot with the real estate agent, before the painters came, and the men with the new carpets. Mrs. Halliday was awfully angry—I can understand why they think she killed her sister. Not that I think so, of course."

"Was there anything you saw that makes you think that?"

"No, just that she seemed like such a nice woman when she wasn't shouting at her sister. She gave me that picture when she was cleaning things up."

That explained the Van Gogh.

"Did Mrs. Hellman have any arguments with anyone else while she was here? That you saw or heard?"

"No. She didn't spend much time here, of course. About once a week, at lunchtime, she would pick Charlie up and they would leave. They were always back within a couple of hours. And she didn't stay."

"What about Charlie? Was he involved in any arguments?"

"Not that I know of. Not that I saw or heard."

That was all she could give me. As I got up to leave, she said, "Let me give you my telephone number—you can call me if you have any more questions. And I'd love to hear about it, if you find anything out."

She left the room and was back a moment later with a slip of paper on which she had written "Mrs. Lewis" and a phone number. No first name. That always bothers me, when women do that. An abbreviated identity, and that of the men they marry, not their own. Things like that make me glad I'm single.

I thanked Mrs. Lewis and said good-bye.

The next stop was City Hall again, property records, to see who owned the house. The owner might be able to tell me something more. And the owner did—although not what I had expected. The owner was Castle Properties, the same closely held corporation in Carson City that had owned the house on Quincy that Mary and Willie moved to. Even though the one on Roberts had been trashed.

And that meant I had some questions for Castle Properties' agent. Fortunately, I already knew who he was: Terry Dickerson, who had sent me Joan Halliday.

"Freddie, I swear to you I don't know a thing," Terry

said when I confronted him in his office fifteen minutes later. His office was on South Virginia, just past the curve of the freeway, a small fake-colonial brick building with a modest sign that said Real Estate and Insurance.

"Come on. These people trash a house owned by people you represent, supposedly disappear, you tell Joan Halliday to hire me to find them, they turn up in another house owned by the same people you represent, and you tell me you don't know a thing?"

"I didn't know they were living in the house on Quincy— really I didn't. I didn't receive instructions to rent it until a couple of months ago, and I had it fixed up and painted— not because it was trashed, just because of normal wear and tear—and I rented it to a black couple with three kids. That must have been after you got the car back, and Mary and Willie moved on to parts unknown."

"You're certain it's 'to parts unknown'?"

"On my honor."

I had to think about that. Terry and I went back to third grade together. He had been a smart kid—always one of the last two or there standing in a spelling bee—and he seemed to be a reasonable adult. He had less blond hair on top of his head than he had in third grade, and considerably more on his chin, and most of his acne had cleared up, but I had no reason to think that the changes were more than skin deep, and therefore no reason to doubt him. Except that I could never understand why such a smart kid had gone into selling real estate and insurance.

"Okay. Then who is Castle Properties and how do I get in touch with them?"

"I don't know, and you probably can't."

"Terry, don't do this to me."

"I know—I know you're in this because I gave your name to Joan Halliday, but I didn't think it was anything more complicated than a simple skip. And if it had been that, you would have owed me. Now that it isn't, you're thinking maybe I owe you."

"No, you don't. And I still owe you for sending me a client. But if you know something that would help Joan Halliday, maybe you owe her."

"I don't."

"What about Castle Properties? You must know something about them—you do work for them."

"I don't know much. I correspond with a post office box. Everything is signed by Irene Martinez, the secretary-treasurer of the corporation. I can give you her telephone number, but I warn you that it's always answered by a machine, and she calls me back."

"Great. How can you do business on that basis?"

"They never give me any hassle and they pay on time."

"Okay. Do you know who the other officers of the corporation are?"

"No."

"Do you know if it's registered in Nevada?"

"I think so."

"Thanks for your help."

He glared. I left.

A friend who works at the phone company had given me a reverse directory for Reno-Sparks and Carson. It was last year's, but I didn't think the number was a new one. I also didn't think it was listed, but it was worth a shot, so I went home and checked. I was right. It wasn't listed. I called and left a message on the answering machine.

When I was a kid, Carson City seemed a long way away. One summer when I was in college, I was doing temporary office work in lieu of any better job offers, and for two weeks I had to commute to a soils engineer's office in Carson. A little over a half hour each way. Interminable. That's a small-town perspective for you.

Then, there was still a lot of open space on 395 South. There's still some, but it's becoming city-to-city trailer courts. I passed the old Palomino Guest Ranch sign as I left the city, a testimonial to the nation's easing divorce laws and the drying up of that part of Nevada's tourist business.

It isn't totally gone—the divorce business, that is, not the Palomino Ranch—but it isn't the same. The sign is the only thing left of the Palomino Guest Ranch. The old white frame house that always looked so inviting is gone, and the land is about to become the next shopping mall. There are so many of those in Reno, too many for its size, and I always wonder who shops there.

As I passed the city limits, everything turned brown. Actually, it turned brown before the city limits—nobody got around to landscaping the area around the freeway, and it looked like what was left after strip miners depart. But south of the city was still claimed by the desert. Part of it was the eternal problem with water in the area, part the season. Autumn and winter in Reno always look like a depression, no matter what the economy is doing. And forget all that poetry about purple sage. I guess sometimes it looks purple in the right light, but most of the time it's a kind of bluish gray, and the rest of the time it's brown.

Something like halfway between Reno and Carson lies Bowers Mansion. It caught my eye that day because it looked as if it had a fresh coat of paint. The Nevada Historical Society strikes again. Sandy Bowers, who built the mansion, was Nevada's first multimillionaire, and his wife, Eilley Orrum Cowan Bowers, was Nevada's first famous divorcee. The Girl Scouts used to visit Bowers Mansion, to use the public pool, which was always scummy. Maybe they still visit, but I haven't been a Girl Scout for years. The fun part of the trip was always sneaking away from the troop and climbing the hills behind the mansion to look at the graves. Eilley Orrum. The sound of that name always fascinated me. Eilley Orrum.

You know you're getting close to Carson when the fast food starts. The town—not even generously can it be called a city—seems several miles long and about three streets wide. It wouldn't exist if it weren't the state capital. The old and the new are juxtaposed precariously. Across the street from the new state senate building is an old brick structure housing a bar that looks as if it opened the day Prohibition was repealed. The Watering Hole it is called and it is that, the place where the political animals go to drink after a long day swinging from the vines.

I turned off the so-called highway, barely four lanes at that point, and parked. Carson is so small it doesn't have to restrict parking. I flipped a mental coin over lunch at the Paiute Inn, Carson City's one hotel-casino of any size, or a fast-food burger. The burger won. I ate it as I walked down the street toward the capitol, where I would find the state Department of Corporations.

A humpbacked woman of sixty or so appraised me severely when I asked to see the records that would tell me who the corporate officers of Castle Properties were. Her eyes were steel, her glasses were steel, her hair was steel, not a wisp out of place. Osteoporosis strikes even the sternest. She limped to a shelf, pulled out a large loose-leaf book, and returned to the counter.

Irene Martinez was the secretary-treasurer, that was no surprise. Someone named Joaquin Meara was the president, whoever he was. The vice president, however, was clearly the important name here. Henry d'Arbanville. Known as Hank. Whoever else he was, he was the eldest son of the family that owned the Paiute Inn, and a state senator. Rumored to be running for the Big Senate in Washington next time around. The address for Castle Properties was still a post office box. I already had the phone number.

I thanked the gnomish creature, who glared suspiciously as she returned the book to its shelf.

The Carson City telephone directory showed no Irene Martinez, no Joaquin Meara, and an address and telephone number for Henry d'Arbanville that was clearly professional. I decided to try the post office box first.

I picked up a copy of *Newsweek* at the corner drugstore, moved my car around to the front of the post office, walked through the small lobby to spot the location of the box, and returned to my car to wait. A couple of people walked through the doors in the course of the afternoon, but they turned toward the windows, not the boxes, and when the front doors were locked at six, I was still sitting there.

What if nobody bothered to check the box unless she (Irene, that is) knew there was something there? Or only checked once a week? I could spend a lot of time reading magazines that Joan Halliday might not want to pay me for.

I walked back to the drugstore—fortunately, since it was on the main drag, it was open until seven—picked up a box of bright red stationery, scrawled "I want to talk with you" on the back of a business card, stuck it in an envelope, stamped it, and mailed it in the box in front of the post office. All things considered, it should be in the Castle Properties box the next day.

No message from Joan Halliday was waiting when I got home, so I decided I was still on the case. I drove back to Carson City the next morning.

Irene Martinez showed up a little after eleven. At least, I thought it was Irene Martinez. I had known her as Irene Rebideaux in the seventh grade. I followed her up the steps to make sure that she was checking the right box, although I stayed so far back that I could only be certain that it was in the right area. I didn't want to talk with her just yet—I wanted an address first. When I saw the flash of a red envelope in her hand, I went back to the car, head down, still keeping out of sight. Irene and I had been on opposite softball teams in seventh-grade phys ed, and she had taunted me about striking out—which I rarely did—once too often. I dropped the bat, walked over, and slugged her so hard she thought I had dislocated her jaw. She was too stunned to hit me back, which I had fully expected her to do. I was sent to the principal's office for fighting—the only time in my school career—but it was worth it. She never taunted me again.

She was as big as I was in the seventh grade, and she still looked big as I watched her walking down the street, getting into the pale blue Mercedes. I wondered who she had married. She was wearing a dress, too, a full-skirted, melon-colored one with a jacket tailored to minimize her broad shoulders, the dress-for-success look. The expensive dress-for-success look.

She drove a couple of blocks and turned into the parking lot of a squat stone building, probably fairly new but pretending to be old. I parked on the street, waited a moment, and followed her in. The directory inside the front door showed several doctors, a law firm, and CP Inc. I climbed the stairs to the third floor. And I changed my mind. The building was really old—the stair rail was old, polished, dark wood, and so were the doors. CP Inc. was right under 301 in softly burnished gold leaf. The door was unlocked, so I walked in.

Irene Rebideaux Martinez was sitting behind a rosewood desk in what was apparently a one-room office, sorting the mail. She hadn't gotten any prettier since seventh grade, and the glare she greeted me with didn't soften her features. Her expensive haircut tried to—the short black curls around her ears and chin had been blown and sprayed by a professional. But her chin was still square, her nose still flat, her eyes still too small for her face. And the mole on her upper lip was still disfiguring.

"Hi, Irene," I said. "How's your jaw?"

"I got your note," she said, holding up my business card. "I didn't expect you so soon."

"Well, I was just at the post office, so I thought I'd drop by."

"What do you want?"

"I'm looking for Mary Yates and Willie Carver."

"Who are they?"

"They were your tenants on Quincy, after they had trashed your house on Roberts, where they were supposed to be taking care of Charlie Barrington."

"I know there was some damage to the house on Roberts after Charlie moved out. But his daughter paid for it. The house on Quincy had been vacant for months until we asked

Terry Dickerson to fix it up and rent it. It's a bad section of town, and it's hard to find trustworthy people to rent to. For a while we simply didn't try. We should probably just sell the property. And I've never heard of—what were their names?''

"Mary Yates and Willie Carver.''

"Yes. So you must have been mistaken about the house on Quincy. They couldn't have been living there. And why would we have rented to someone who had already trashed one of our houses?''

"I wondered that, too, Irene.''

I walked to the window and looked out. She hadn't asked me to sit, and since the only chair besides hers was a low, fat, upholstered one to the right of the desk, squeezed against the file cabinets that were the only other furniture, I hadn't wanted to. The street was quiet, no cars, no pedestrians. I turned back.

"How much property do you own, anyway? I mean—is it little enough that you know all your tenants? I had guessed there was more than that.''

She flushed, turning her olive skin an interesting shade of maroon.

"I don't have to answer that. This isn't a public corporation. I don't have to answer any of your questions.''

"What happens if I tell the police I suspect someone was dealing drugs out of one of your houses?''

She laughed.

"What happens? Nothing. They ask you for proof and you go away.''

"What about newspapers? Suppose I discuss this with someone at the Nevada *Herald*?''

She shrugged.

"Suppose you do. Same thing happens. There are libel laws, and the *Herald* won't print allegations. You can't threaten me, Freddie.'' She twitched a smile. "And I don't think you'll hit me.''

I wanted to. Badly.

"This time I'd charge you with assault," she added.

"Well, I guess I just struck out."

"Again."

I left as gracefully as I could. Also as quickly.

Nevada never had a state speed limit, and the Highway Patrol is pretty selective about enforcing the federally imposed one. I was still lucky that nobody saw me screaming back to Reno. She was right, of course—I didn't have enough to take to anybody. Besides, I still didn't think this was about drugs. I was going to have to come from another direction.

I calmed down enough to realize that it had been a while since I had checked on Stephanie Johnson, so I drove by the last address I had for her. Somehow it didn't surprise me to find another family in that house.

When I got home, I called my buddy in welfare and asked him to check for a new address for Stephanie Johnson. Then I called the charter service and arranged for the Cherokee 180 that I liked to think of as mine. I would have to take a look at the Las Vegas connections.

Chapter
5

I'VE NEVER LIKED Las Vegas, and I didn't look forward to flying there. Flying I looked forward to—always—but not Las Vegas. Reno-Vegas is one of those north-south cross-state rivalries, something like San Francisco and Los Angeles. Or even North and South Tahoe. Growing up in Reno, the old money, dude ranch, hunting and fishing, Biggest Little City in the world, I learned to see Las Vegas as the parvenu, trying to take advantage of its new people and new money to control the state, much to the detriment of the sparsely populated Cow Counties that held most of the territory—or what wasn't owned by the federal government, anyway.

And UNR was and would always be *the* University of Nevada for me. It might have remained so for the rest of the world had it not been for the government scientists in the southern part of the state who felt they ought to have a university around. A couple of casino owners felt the need for sports and culture—especially basketball—and the rest, as they say, is UNLV history.

Las Vegas, like Reno, is a split town. The reality of either place depends on where you live and work. Each has a real city with variations in wealth rivaling Beverly Hills and Watts, a real university community, and a wide-open tourist center of flashy hotels and flashier casinos. Vegas actually has two: Downtown and the Strip.

55

The differences between Las Vegas and Reno today: Vegas is bigger and flatter, and still newer, always newer. I think the real city is harder to find, but that may be because I'm just not there enough. And there are plastic palm trees at the airport—the big one, McCarran International, named for a dead senator best known for his xenophobia, not the small charter terminal next to it that I was heading for.

I got up in the slow haze of dawn, angering two cats who had expected another hour of undisturbed sleep, and drove to the small charter terminal just south of Reno-Cannon International (honoring another former senator with a less than distinguished record) to pick up the blue and white Cherokee that I took up whenever I could. I parked close to the glass doors of the small building, almost alone in the parking lot.

"Hey, Freddie," the man behind the counter said as I walked in.

"Hey, Jerry," I responded automatically.

Jerry McIntire and I were always a little stiff with each other—his older brother had been the one real love of my life, and it embarrassed him to see me. He never volunteered information about Rob and Thelma and the kids, for which I was grateful, and I never asked, for which Jerry was doubtless equally grateful.

I signed for the Cherokee with a minimum of conversation. The walkaround was routine—I drained the fuel sumps, checked the tires, propeller, oil level, fuel tanks, control surfaces, and finally disconnected the tie-downs.

Inside and ready to go, I picked up the microphone.

"Reno Ground Clearance, this is November eight-one-nine-four Whiskey, requesting straight-out departure to the southeast, direct to Las Vegas."

"Ninety-four Whiskey, squawk, oh-one-seven-four contact, departure one-two-six point three when airborne."

"Ready to taxi, with the numbers."

I finally took off into the rising sun, a bright, blinding shock above the smog line, and circled around to the south.

If you've ever dreamed you were flying, soaring over treetops and swooping down to skim the earth, balancing between earth and sky, you have a sense of what it's like to pilot your own plane. People who have a fear of flying in a commercial plane are just being sensible—not only do they give up control over their own fate, they don't even know who they're handing it over to. But when you're in your own plane, when your hands are the ones on the controls, you are close to total freedom. It's like dancing with a partner who never lets your feet touch the ground, but who nevertheless lets you lead. I've loved it from the first time I discovered the way a plane responds to touch—not heavily like a car, but lightly, more like a musical instrument. Albeit a loud one. I'm still surprised at how much I can hear through ear plugs, how easy it is to filter out the engine and still hear the radio.

My flight plans are never quite direct. I was taught—and I still think it's a good rule—to chart the flight from airport to airport, Yerington, Hawthorne, Coaldale, Indian Springs, until I reached Las Vegas. I'd never had to land suddenly, but part of the thrill of flying is contingency planning, the feeling that nobody but me is here in a crisis. I skirted the Sierras for the first part of the trip, then headed southeast over dry, potato-skin desert.

Flying yourself takes three times as long. It's thirty times as much fun.

Las Vegas arises suddenly from the desert, particularly during the day, when there is no neon to advertise it. I heard Joseph Campbell on television once, talking about the fact that medieval cities could first be spotted by the church spires, but modern cities were dominated by office buildings, signifying the changing places in society of Church and Business. In Las Vegas, the tall buildings are all hotel casinos. The dominance of the con game.

By the time I landed, the rest of the world had settled into its midmorning routine—a hot, dry, Las Vegas-in-September midmorning. Cabdrivers, secretaries, real estate agents, casino operators, dealers of all sorts, cops, prostitutes, professors, athletes, day creatures up and about, night creatures asleep.

My first stop—I barely got the plane tied down first—was the women's room. The thermos of coffee I carried in the plane had hardly paused in my bloodstream before heading out. That, of course, is the major disadvantage of flying your own plane. Men may be able to relieve themselves in flight without too much mess. I haven't been able to figure out an alternative to waiting.

My second stop was the McCarran terminal's rent-a-car counter, where Lurene's clone gave me a car without glancing up. She would never be able to recognize me again. If I had signed Joan Halliday—and given the appropriate credit card—I could have gotten away with murder.

I realize that it's no longer fashionable to complain about Japanese cars—with justice, of course, since in many cases they're better values than their American counterparts. But that still rankles, and I almost complained when she gave me the keys to the Toyota. I've owned Fords ever since I could drive, and I've never had a lemon.

I tried to call Joan Halliday, let her know I was in town, but only the machine answered. Since I planned to drive out to Echo Bay anyway, I hoped I might find her at the houseboat.

But first I drove into town to find Aunt Mae. I picked up Interstate 15 and skipped the Strip. Never look at the Strip during the day. It looks like a stage set forlornly waiting for the actors, with just a few puzzled members of the audience wandering around. The address I had was not far from Fremont Street, and I had to see a bit of downtown. Like the Strip, but worse. Seedier.

As I passed Aunt Mae's house, I wondered whether stopping and going in was a good call. All large cities have areas right around the corner from downtown that suddenly turn weird. You can be right in the heart of the tourist section in LA, San Francisco, or Washington, DC, and suddenly you make a wrong turn and feel as if you've just entered the Twilight Zone. Aunt Mae lived on one of those streets. Two blocks from neon, and it looked like Beirut. Boards where windows used to be, graffiti on peeling paint. Too hot to be inside, too dangerous to be outside. No one in sight. I decided to risk it.

I rang the doorbell. I didn't hear anything, guessed it didn't work, and knocked. Then I pounded.

The woman who opened the door a crack, less than the length of the chain lock, looked like a black Mrs. Lewis.

"What you want?" she asked.

There would be no offer of coffee here, and truth wouldn't open any doors.

"I'm looking for Mary Yates," I said. "I hope you might help me find her."

"There ain't no Mary Yates here."

She continued to peer through the narrow opening.

I pulled out my card and handed it to her.

"I'm looking for Mary Yates at the request of an attorney. Someone she used to take care of died, and it seems she was mentioned in his will."

I let her look at the card, then continued.

"If you know how to find her, you might ask her to get in touch with me."

"Who died? What will?"

"I'm afraid I can't tell you that. Particularly since there's no Mary Yates here."

She slammed the door in my face.

I was relieved to get out of there. Maybe I would have done better if I hadn't stopped, if I had talked Deke into coming to Vegas, let him talk to her. She had no reason to trust me. Neither would Mary Yates when she heard about me. And I was certain she would hear about me.

The air-conditioning on the Toyota worked. I would say that for it. And I needed it. Las Vegas can hit a hundred even into October—and then drop to forty at night. You want desert? You got it. I headed south on Fremont, which turns into Boulder Highway, and I was quickly in it. I saw a sign welcoming me to Henderson, Growing Toward Tomorrow, near a large junk pile and a couple of trailers and thought this was someone's idea of a desert joke, but I discovered that there actually was a small, spunky outpost of civilization about ten miles later. Henderson had big ideas.

I turned onto Lake Mead Boulevard, then North Shore Boulevard, increasingly convinced that there was no lake anywhere, that Lake Mead was an elaborate hoax, a mass illusion, perhaps a mirage that only appears at certain times of the year. The Boat Storage and Bait and Tackle signs that popped up occasionally apropos of nothing were just part of the joke. I like the desert as much as anyone, I think, or I wouldn't live in Reno, but this one was failing to attract me. It was the same tawny sand covered with scrub that covers most of the state, with the same purple-brown mountains that always appear deceptively close. I've thought that's how the settlers made it across the desert in the Conestogas, because the purple-brown mountains always appeared deceptively close. And, of course, that's why some of the Conestogas didn't make it across—the mountains weren't close at all. And neither was the lake. The flatness of the terrain was occasionally broken by amazingly bright, striated red rock formations, hints at the grandeur of the Valley of Fire, a few miles to the north. They looked as if God had been playing at making Easter Island statues, and dropped a few when they didn't come out quite the way He wanted, and I thought how right Walter Van Tilburg Clark had been when he sang of the unfinished land of Nevada.

I had caught a few glimpses of water before I reached the turnoff to Echo Bay, so I knew there really was a lake somewhere. I had expected the terrain to change as I got closer, but of course it didn't. Not even a saguaro cactus, one of the natural signposts to nowhere, that grace the deserts farther south. And man-made lakes don't have beaches, just edges.

I drove past the park ranger's station, past the cluster of mobile homes, around the Echo Bay Inn, which was nothing more than an overdecorated motel, and pulled into the parking lot near the marina. A few of the blue and white rental houseboats were in the cove south of the dock and a breakwater that appeared to have been constructed from old truck tires. More were in their slips.

Joan Halliday's houseboat was the Queen of Hearts, and I walked out on the pier, looking down each of the gated docks, thinking I might find her on the boat. But I couldn't find it. That would explain, of course, why I hadn't heard from her for the last couple of days. One more time, she had taken the houseboat out on the lake, to get away from everybody.

Rudy Stapp, the PI, had told me to check with the man at the Echo Bay tackle shop. But I needed to stretch my legs first, walk out the cramp of the airplane and the car. I remembered that I hadn't put anything but coffee in my stomach since dawn, so I bought a hot dog and a Coke from a food stand and sat down at the scratched wood picnic table to eat. The air was fresh, a comfortable eighty degrees. I wanted to take my shirt off and wade into the lake. Instead, I rested a moment, watching the boats and the water skiers, careless grasshoppers in the Indian summer.

The tackle shop was at the base of the long pier, which was studded with fishing boats as well as houseboats. The sign over the door identified the proprietor—Lucas Hecht. He was just outside the door, leaning against the jamb and looking out over the lake, a heavyset, fortyish man, wearing a plaid cotton shirt and white T-shirt with his jeans that were more than the day required. Overweight men do that, for some reason. He had an open face, wide features framed by gray hair and a trimmed gray beard. He watched me walk up, and nodded when I stopped in front of him. He was maybe an inch shorter than I am. Usually when I walk right up to a man like that, he'll stand up straighter, or back off a little. This one didn't.

I introduced myself, and reminded him that Rudy Stapp had stopped by to see him on Joan Halliday's behalf.

He nodded again, regarding me through bifocals with heavy black frames. Something about him made me uncomfortable. He wasn't that good-looking, but I was aware of him as a man, and I couldn't figure out why. I backed up a step.

"You do know Mrs. Halliday?" I asked.

"Of course I do. Queen of Hearts, white with green trim."

"What?"

"Her houseboat." He smiled with such good humor that I smiled in return. "Come on in."

I followed him into the small tackle shop.

"Want a beer?" he asked, pulling two cans out of an ice chest behind a counter taken up mostly by a very large, old-fashioned cash register, the kind with all the silver curlicues.

"Sure."

The cans weren't quite cold enough. They sprayed as he popped the tops. He held out one of the wet cans. His hand was large and weathered. I was careful not to touch it.

I took a sip, then another. Beer really is better than coke on a warm afternoon.

"I understand you saw Mrs. Halliday on the day her sister was murdered. Is that right?"

"Well, not quite."

He leaned against the cooler, consuming about a quarter of his can in one gulp.

"What did you see?" I prompted.

"I saw her boat—her boat was out on the lake, just the way it is now."

"How can you be so sure you have the time right?"

"Because I saw it in the paper—we do have newspapers here, you know, and everybody in the state knows who Charlie Barrington is. The day I read about the murder, I looked out on the lake, and the Queen of Hearts was there, and it had been there for a day or two. I can't tell you how long. But I remembered wondering when she was going to come in, and who was going to tell her, or if she had heard it first on the radio. That's one of the problems of fame, you know. Remember the old lieutenant governor, Rex Bell, the cowboy star? When he had a heart attack and died in his girlfriend's arms, his son found out about it watching television. I know—I was there—the poor fellow was destroyed, hearing about his dad like that. I hoped that wouldn't happen to Mrs. Halliday—and it would have been worse, since her sister was murdered."

"When did Mrs. Halliday's boat come in?" I had heard the Rex Bell story before, but you never know what's rumor and what's truth, particularly when it happened thirty years or so ago. Which made Lucas Hecht awfully young at the time. I filed a mental note to stay skeptical.

"Sometime that evening. It was still out when I left for the day, but it was back in its slip the next morning. She has a radio on board—I figured her husband called her in."

"How do you know she was out there alone?"

"I don't know for a fact. But she's usually out there alone. She's the one who likes the boat and the lake, not her husband. Sometimes during the winter she's almost the only person out there."

"Could she have left the boat, flown to Reno, killed her sister, flown back to Las Vegas, and then returned to the boat without you being aware of it?"

He laughed, almost spraying me with beer. He wiped his mouth on his sleeve. I wondered why he was nervous.

"Well, you know, I thought about that, after I read she'd been accused. I suppose she could have swum ashore at night, dried off and changed somewhere, flown to Reno, killed her sister, flown back to Las Vegas, changed somewhere, and swum back to the boat. But it just doesn't sound like her."

I didn't know whether it sounded like her or not. But I did wonder why somebody would go to all that trouble to establish an alibi and then sign her own name on a form at a rent-a-car counter.

"One more question. Your glasses. How can you be so sure which boat was out there?"

He took off the glasses and handed them to me. I put them on, still careful not to touch him. The bottoms were a blur, but the tops were plain. Nonprescription.

"I'm farsighted. I could get half glasses, or reading glasses, but I have to do so much close work that it's easier to have them on all the time. Or most of the time, anyway. Want to go outside and see how many boats I can name from the shore?"

"No, I believe you. Thanks."

I finished the beer and put the can on the counter.

"Anytime." He nodded. "Drop on by."

I walked to the end of the pier and looked for the Queen of Hearts. I couldn't read the name, but there was a green and white houseboat maybe a half mile out. Having come this far—being this close—seeing the boat—I wasn't willing to leave without talking to Joan Halliday. I thought about finding a ship-to-shore radio, but I wasn't sure how to call her if I found one. The boat was clearly too far for me to swim—Mick Halliday's youthful efforts notwithstanding, I am not that good. I decided to rent an outboard and motor out.

Lucas Hecht was still standing in the door to the tackle shop.

"Where's the nearest place to rent a boat?" I asked.

"You want to talk to her? I'll take you."

That was nice—maybe she should hear from him that she really did have an alibi. He locked the door to the tackle shop and hung a sign with a clock that said "BACK AT . . ." on it. He set the time for an hour. We walked back down the pier, and he unlocked the gate to Dock D. He stopped in front of a small speedboat.

"Here she is—The Fearless Leaker."

He hopped onto the boat, gracefully for a man of his size,

and held out his hand. I thought about disdaining it, but he was doing me a favor. I took it and followed him. The hand felt okay, but I dropped it as soon as I could.

Speedboats are maybe the second loudest things on earth, next to airplanes. I don't know why fishermen bother with Lake Mead, except that it's big enough that the motor sounds must dissipate. Or maybe Lake Mead fish get used to noise, unlike fish at older, natural lakes.

We reached the Queen of Hearts in minutes.

"Ahoy, Queen of Hearts," Lucas Hecht called as he cut the motor.

There was no sign of life. And she must have heard us.

"Ahoy, Queen of Hearts," he called again.

"Get close enough for me to climb aboard," I told him.

He didn't question me. He maneuvered closer to the anchored houseboat. The engine gave two little spurts and died, and Lucas Hecht tossed the looped end of a rope over a post sticking up from the deck of the houseboat. He used the rope to pull us closer. I grabbed the rope and the post and crawled aboard.

"Mrs. Halliday?"

No answer.

"Mrs. Halliday? Are you okay? It's me, Freddie O'Neal."

No answer.

The door to the cabin was open. There really wasn't much of a living space, not much more than a double bunk, a sink, a refrigerator, a hot plate, a couple of cabinets, a built-in table, and a door that probably led to a toilet and shower. But it was the bottom bunk, of course. That's where she was, lying on top of a green and white striped blanket. She was wearing faded denims, deck shoes, and a gray sweatshirt, a comfortable kind of outfit for hanging out on a houseboat. Her legs were out straight, the top part of her body turned, arms over the edge of the bed, as if she had been trying to get up but hadn't made it. I didn't need to touch her to know she was dead.

Chapter
6

I WANTED TO cry. I wanted to huddle on the floor with my chin against my chest and my hands around my knees and sob. Part of me wondered vaguely what I was to Hecuba or Hecuba to me that I should weep for her. But I wanted to. I had known her, known what she was like alive, and I didn't want to think of her dying here alone, reaching for help, when there was no one to reach back.

"Is everything okay?"

I could hear Lucas Hecht clambering onto the houseboat.

"No. No, it isn't okay," I called.

I walked out to stop him, stop him from going inside where Joan Halliday's body was cramped in death.

"What is it? What's wrong?"

I watched him turn white, and I knew it was because of the expression on my face.

"She's dead. I'll wait with her while you go for help."

Help.

"Oh, God, no. Let me see her."

He pushed past me into the cabin, stopping just inside the door, where he could see the dangling arm. He slumped, leaned against the wall for a moment, then turned back to me.

"Are you—?" He raised one hand, tentatively.

I nodded, cutting off the gesture. There wasn't an alternative.

He stumbled into his boat, started the engine, and sped off, leaving a faint, oily slick on the water, almost a rainbow in the sunlight. I turned away, not ready for any ambiguous signs of hope.

I walked back inside. I stuck my hands in my pockets, so I wouldn't touch something by mistake. The tears started running down my face as I looked around. I wasn't exactly crying—I just couldn't stop the tears.

I tried to look at the body, wanted to come to some conclusion about how she died, but I couldn't do it. Most of my cases are run-of-the-mill, not murder. This was the first time I had seen a dead person who hadn't been all prettied up for the funeral, and I wasn't handling it very well. I had to look at everything else instead.

The cabin was neat, no real signs of occupancy, and that bothered me. Most people slop around when they go off by themselves, or at least I think they do, maybe because I do. But then, I slop around even at home. This was a home to Joan Halliday, and maybe she always put everything in its place. And maybe on a boat, where there's so little room anyway, people tend to be neater. The small, four-burner stove was clean, a teakettle sitting on a back burner. Nothing in the tiny sink. Nothing on the counter, not even a coffee cup. Cupboard doors were closed. If the body hadn't been there, I would have opened them—the edge of a finger on the side of a knob wouldn't have messed up any evidence. But I felt it would have been an invasion of her privacy, and she had so little left.

A speedboat roared by, gently rocking the Queen of Hearts in its wake.

The clunk of a bottle falling brought me back to the narrow bunk. It was Jack Daniel's, tightly corked, and it had landed on a rug, so I didn't bother to pick it up. There was a fresh-looking brown stain on the rug. I knelt down and touched it. Still damp. And the whiskey odor was so strong that I was surprised I hadn't smelled it earlier. A glass was wedged underneath the bunk, maybe knocked there by another speedboat, the likely source of the stain. And if Joan Halliday had been alive when it fell, she would surely have picked it up.

Behind the glass, in the corner, I saw what looked like a small, brown-plastic prescription bottle. I was debating whether to reach for it when I heard the roar of another speedboat stop abruptly. And then voices, and someone coming aboard.

I was on my feet, more or less composed, as they entered the cabin.

I introduced myself to the park ranger, a very young, pleasant-looking man who looked as frightened as I felt. I showed him my ID, told him why I was there, promised him I hadn't touched anything. He nodded.

"Lucas is waiting outside for you, said he'd take you back. I called the state police in Overton, and they'll have a boat coming out. Do you think you might stay around for a few hours? I'm sure they'll have some questions after they've checked the place out."

I had planned on flying back to Reno in the evening, but I was too tired. Besides, I would have to see Mick before I left. And I didn't want to call him until after I had talked with the police. I couldn't afford it, but I would have to spend the night in Echo Bay.

"I'll stay," I told him. "I'll take a room. I'll be either there or in the bar."

I don't normally drink much except for an occasional beer, but I thought this might be time for an exception.

The ranger nodded again.

"We'll catch up with you."

Lucas Hecht was standing, staring out at the water when I left the cabin. I was relieved to be outside. I wasn't sure how long I hadn't been breathing, but I knew I needed a deep one.

I let him help me into The Fearless Leaker. Neither of us spoke on the way back to the pier.

"How well did you know her?" I asked as we walked

along the shore that wasn't a beach. As he was tying up his boat a tacit understanding had somehow been made, that we were both shaken by the experience, that we wanted to walk a little. An instant pseudo-intimacy, because we were alive and she was dead.

"I was going to ask you that," he said. "I didn't know her very well, really—not what you'd call knowing somebody. I saw her several times a year—I've lived here a little less than three years—and I liked the way she looked, strong and capable, as if she could take care of herself, but still pretty. She was friendly, neighborly, but we never talked beyond the weather. You?"

"Well—she hired me, and we talked a little, I guess, but I didn't know her either. I wish I had—I remember her, years ago at the Sierra Madre, when she danced."

I remember long legs, pink feathers, and death.

"Want a beer?"

"Sure."

What I didn't want was to be by myself in a motel room thinking about Joan Halliday alone and dying, found by two people who barely knew her. And I didn't want to think about being the one to tell Mick.

We didn't go back to the tackle shop. We went to another houseboat, larger than the Queen of Hearts, once painted white, but now a pale, flaking gray. Lucas Hecht was not compulsively neat. But the place was cleaner than a lot of bachelor pads—in fact, it was cleaner than mine usually is, certainly cleaner than mine was likely to be if I had an unexpected guest.

This time, the beer was cold. We sat out on the deck, in a couple of canvas chairs, looking at the lake and the mountains as we drank. And one led to a fourth. Neither one of us talked much. He was kind of a nice guy, Lucas Hecht. Usually I'm not very comfortable with men, but he was easy to be with. As we finished each beer I thought about leaving, and then I didn't do it. I didn't want to be alone.

"I have to go," I said, forcing myself, as he reached for

a fifth beer. "I have to talk to the police, and to Mick, and I told the ranger I'd be at the Echo Bay Inn."

"The police'll find you. It's a small cove."

I giggled. The beer, the stress, and the heat of the afternoon were floating through my head.

"I feel really grubby. I've been up since dawn, and my client's dead, and I want to take a bath."

"Well—I can't offer you a bath, but I've got a shower."

The offer—and I was so out of it that it took me a few seconds to realize just what kind of offer it was—dangled there between us. And I didn't know what to do. I had been sleeping alone for so long that I must have renewed my virginity several full moons ago. On the other hand, this wasn't exactly your usual first date. He held out his hand.

"I'd really like it if you stayed," he said.

People do funny things under stress, things they wouldn't do under normal circumstances. And there was something about the sight of death that had made me want to reaffirm my connection to life. Touching somebody seemed the most likely way. I had only been to bed with two men, and one was a rebound from the other, and neither relationship had started fast. Still, I decided I liked the way his hand looked—and the way it felt—and I took it.

The shower was barely big enough for both of us. But we soaped and scrubbed and shampooed each other, and somehow it worked.

The bed wasn't much bigger, but we made that work, too.

The knocking—the heavy knocking—on the door woke both of us. A soft, gray twilight barely lit the room. I had slept just long enough for the beer to give me a headache, and the knocking reverberated against my skull.

"Just a minute," Lucas yelled.

He grabbed one of the towels we had dropped on the floor, wrapped it around his waist, and opened the door a crack. There was mumbling, I couldn't quite understand it.

He shut the door and came back.

"Tom—the ranger—and a state cop. I told them to come back in an hour."

"Oh, God," I moaned. "What're they going to think?"

Lucas grinned.

"Whatever they want, I guess."

The second time it worked even better. I've never understood the jokes about women who avoid sex because of a headache. It sure cured mine. And by the time the state policeman returned, this time without the ranger, we were both dressed, drinking yet another beer, and Lucas was checking to see what there was to go with a couple of grilled striped bass for dinner.

The state policeman was Sgt. Morrison. He was six feet tall, square-shouldered and square-jawed, with the dead steely eyes of a born cop. We walked to the end of the dock, not to interfere with Lucas at the small circular barbecue on the deck of the houseboat.

I didn't see any reason to complicate things by getting into Castle Properties or drugs, but I told him most of the rest.

"Sounds like she was unbalanced," he said. "This one will probably come up accidental overdose at the coroner's inquest."

"Why? What did you find?"

"She had a prescription for Valium, and it looks like she mixed a few too many with her Jack Daniel's. Nobody'll want to call it suicide—especially when she had hired you to prove her innocent of her sister's murder, and everybody else was saying she did it when she was temporarily insane. Temporary insanity'll probably cover this, too."

"It'll cover it—but is it the truth?"

He looked at me as if I might be nuts, as if I might be the next one found curled up dead in a houseboat.

"Probably as close as we'll get to it."

I was going to have to think about that another time.

"What about Mick?"

"We've called him, and he's driving out to Overton—

that's where the body is, the coroner's office in Overton. He'll have to identify her, of course, even though you did already."

I looked away. I hated how relieved I was that I wouldn't have to tell Mick she was dead.

"Is something wrong?"

"No," I lied. "I'll have to talk to him, but I guess I can wait until tomorrow."

"Doesn't seem any point in meeting him in Overton, unless you were a lot closer to the family than you said."

"No, no point. If you see him, tell him I'll call tomorrow."

He nodded. I told him I was flying back to Reno after I talked to Mick, and he seemed to think that was all right. I gave him my card, in case he needed to reach me for the coroner's inquest. He left, and I went back inside.

A tossed salad in a wooden bowl sat on the small table. I could smell garlic bread heating in the toaster oven. Best of all, I could smell the fish. People who complain about the smell of fish have never smelled truly fresh fish, caught in the morning, grilled over hot coals and basted with a little butter that evening.

"He think you did it?"

I had to laugh.

"No, of course he didn't. That isn't even funny."

"But you laughed."

"Yeah, because it was dumb, not because it was funny. But that's okay. I guess it's a dumb night."

"No, it's not. Don't think of it like that."

I did think of it like that. I had to think of it like that, because I didn't know how else to think of it. But he was being nice to me, and actually, as I looked at him, he had cleaned up pretty good. I thought about keeping an open mind, maybe taking this seriously. I was feeling wary, though. And just sober enough to start regretting my impulsiveness. I wasn't sure how long I wanted to stay.

He pulled the foil-wrapped garlic bread out of the toaster oven, tossed it onto the table, and slid the bass onto a couple of white plastic plates with a dark blue geometric pattern.

"Thanks," I said.

I've never been good at this sort of thing, whatever it was, and I sure didn't know how to carry on a casual dinner conversation. So I left it up to him. He didn't seem to know how to hold one, either. We ate a little, and we glanced at each other, and it was awkward.

"Like to go fishing?"

"What?" I was startled, when he finally said something.

"I thought maybe you'd like to go fishing with me tomorrow morning."

"I don't know. I mean, I haven't gone fishing since I was a kid."

I thought of a fish, struggling on a hook at the end of a line, eyes dying, and I knew I couldn't go, not then at least. I had to mess the head and tail up to keep eating the one on my plate, and that was only because I was hungry. And it tasted good. But I had trouble with that dead eye looking at me.

"Want to go?"

"Maybe some other time. I have bad memories of fishing—for some reason I attract mosquitoes, even if I spray. Besides, I have to talk to Mick Halliday tomorrow. And then I have to get back to Reno. I have to get the plane back, and my cats have to be fed."

He wanted to know about the plane and the cats, and that made talking a little easier.

I thought about leaving, going to the Echo Bay Inn for the rest of the night, but that seemed a little silly. I stayed, and we made love again, but by then I was sober enough to be scared and it wasn't as good.

When I woke up the next morning, there was fresh, boiled coffee in a blue and white enamel pot on the stove. Lucas was gone. He had left a note on the table.

"Good luck. Call me if you want to."

That was all it said.

I had to take a shower and get dressed and find Mick

Halliday, and I decided to think about Lucas later, when I got back to Reno.

Sometime during the night the Queen of Hearts had been returned to its slip, which was just a couple of spaces down from Lucas's houseboat. Second Chance. That was the name of Lucas's houseboat. I hadn't seen it the night before.

A man—Mick—was standing on the far side of the Queen of Hearts, a mug of coffee in his hand, staring out across the lake. He turned when I called and motioned me aboard.

"Mick, I'm sorry—" I began.

"Not your fault, Freddie. Nothing you could do. Want some coffee?"

"Yeah, thanks."

I was surprised that he was there, wondered how he could have slept on the Queen of Hearts. But, of course, Joan's body had been gone. He had seen it in Overton. And it probably made sense to stay where he was, rather than going back to the house in Las Vegas. Probably there were things to do, arrangements to make, and it was better that he was close.

I stayed on the deck while he got the coffee.

"I'm glad you stopped by," he said as he came back out on the deck.

The mug Mick gave me was blue and white enamel, just like the one I had been drinking from at Luke's. Probably half the houseboats on the lake used the same blue and white enamel mugs. I took it from him quickly. Mick's hand was shaking.

His face was flushed, sagging, his age was showing in a way it hadn't before, and his white polo shirt and khaki trousers looked as if he had slept in them. I figured they were what he was wearing when the police called him. And he had taken his own car, and the reason he stayed at the boat was that he was too drunk to drive home.

"I was going to call you," I told him. "I wanted to see you before I went back to Reno."

"Ah, Freddie, thanks. But I'm okay. This has been

coming for a long time, and I've known it. That's why I wanted you out of it, when I came to see you in Reno. She's been depressed, depressed about her father, depressed about her life, depressed about I don't know what. And drinking, too. Joan never drank much, until this past year. I've thought maybe she was drinking when she flew to Reno, rented that car, and killed Lois, that maybe she really couldn't remember what happened. Maybe it was all part of the nightmare of her depression.''

''Was she seeing anybody—about her depression?''

''She saw a psychologist once or twice—I told the police about him—but it didn't seem to help. I'm sure they'll talk to him, Freddie. And there's nothing more you can do.''

''Well, yeah, I'm sure they'll talk to him.''

And I was sure the verdict would come back that she had committed suicide while she was depressed, maybe because she had realized she had killed her sister, despite her previous denial. Even though there was no note. I was there, and I would have seen a note. No, not suicide. Morrison had said accidental overdose, that's what it would be.

''And I don't want you hurt by this. I know you've run up some expenses, and I want you to be okay.''

He took a folded piece of paper out of his pants pocket, and stuck it in my shirt.

''Don't look at it now—just take it.''

I pulled it out and looked at it. It was a check for five thousand dollars.

''Mick, I can't take this. I really can't.''

''Sure you can. You shouldn't have been in this in the first place, and you've had expenses, and God knows the stress of finding Joan dead like that, when she was your client. You've earned it, Freddie, you've earned it.''

I didn't know what to do. I put the check back in my shirt, figuring it was one more thing I could think about later. I finished my coffee and said good-bye. Mick had a flash of his old charm as he kissed me on the cheek.

Chapter 7

I DIDN'T DEPOSIT the check. I couldn't bring myself to do it. I thought about it the whole flight back—when I wasn't thinking of Lucas Hecht—and I couldn't deposit the check. Deke called me a fool, said I was well out of it, I should take the money, and I still couldn't deposit the check. I couldn't come up with the right letter to send it back with, either.

I had it out on my desk, and I was sitting staring at it, four days later, when the phone rang.

"Could you possibly stop by my office at the university this afternoon?" Professor Hellman asked.

I told him I'd be there at three.

"Perhaps I shouldn't involve you in this," he said, once I had seated myself in the straight-backed wooden chair beside the desk. Not too comfortable. Can't have students sitting there too long.

The office was almost unchanged since my last visit. The stacks of papers and magazines had grown, however. Papers seem to reproduce like rabbits during the semester.

"I'm involved already—Mrs. Halliday involved me."

"Yes, but Mick told me that he uninvolved you, that he paid you for your time and expenses."

"I haven't cashed the check."

"Ah. Well. As you know, a student of history is a seeker

of truth, and I feel that there is some truth in this story that hasn't yet come to light.''

''What happened, Professor?''

''Two things, really. One was the celerity with which Joan was dispatched. There was no investigation. Just what appeared to be a common agreement to call it accidental overdose and keep it quiet. I called Mick to ask him about the service, see what I could do, and he told me there wouldn't be one. She was cremated yesterday morning. It's so sadly impersonal—as if she had no family, no friends. As if she hadn't had a life. Someone should mourn her, and I suppose this is my way of doing so.''

''Well, okay, but what makes you think it wasn't an accidental overdose?''

''It might have been, of course. Although it doesn't seem like Joan at all.''

''Mick told me she was depressed, seeing a therapist.''

Professor Hellman raised his eyebrows in surprise.

''Was she? This is the first I've heard of it. I suppose that would put a different light on it.''

''Do you want to change your mind about hiring me?''

''No. That's not enough to convince me. I told you there were two things. The other is that I talked to Charlie, and he's scared. I've never seen Charlie scared, in all the years I've known him. He experienced some anxiety over Lois's mishap, but it wasn't really the same thing. I'm sure it doesn't carry much weight with you that I don't believe Joan committed suicide, even accidentally, any more than I believed she murdered Lois. Denial is part of the human condition, particularly when constructs like 'murder' and 'suicide' are operative. I could be denying an obvious truth because it makes me uncomfortable. And one could pose the same argument where Charlie is concerned—of course he wouldn't want to believe that Joan killed Lois and then herself. But denial wouldn't frighten Charlie. Something else has, and I am not someone he would confide in.''

''Why would he confide in me?''

"He might not. I don't know why he would. But even if he doesn't, you might discover the bugbear. A particularly deadly one, in this instance. Before you agree, however, I must tell you that I can't afford to pay you a lot. I thought—if you are willing to do a little exploring—that I would give you a check to cover a few hours of your time, and when it runs out, you could stop. Let me know what you've learned, and if it doesn't seem fruitful to continue, we give up."

"Give up? Just stand back and let the ball roll down the hill?"

"Ah, yes, I suppose your work does sometimes strike you as a Sisyphean task, one that must be repeated, and never ends. The struggle of good against evil. I can easily see it as such."

I was embarrassed. "I didn't mean to phrase it in such epic terms. Besides, Camus said we must imagine Sisyphus happy—and I'm sure not happy about all this."

"Yes. But Sisyphus was a hero, and few of us are heroes."

"I'm not even pretending to be a hero. But I will see what I can find out. And if I can't keep the ball from rolling back down the hill, I'll let you know."

"Fine."

"Since I'm back on the case, there are a couple of things you might help me with. The first is Mary Yates. Who hired her to take care of Charlie?"

He sighed.

"I don't know. I'm afraid I tuned out Lois's problems with Charlie years ago. I have no idea when or how Mary Yates entered the picture. Do you think all this is related to the drugs found in the car?"

"I don't know. But I'd like to talk to Mary Yates. The other question is about Castle Properties. Have you ever heard of them?"

"I'm sorry, but I haven't."

I sighed.

"Okay. I'll let you know what I find out."

The check he gave me was a fraction of what I got from Mick. But it was the excuse I needed to send Mick's check back, with a note saying that even after considerable deliberation, I couldn't accept it.

I left the university, picked up the freeway, and drove to the Golden Age Convalescent Hospital.

Mrs. Schueller was once again on guard, like Cerberus at the gate. Fortunately, she was on the phone, so I threw her a wave of my hand and slid past.

Charlie was in bed, and the TV was silent. I tiptoed in, not wanting to wake him. But he wasn't asleep. He was lying there eyes open, staring at the ceiling. I stepped over to the dresser and knocked gently.

"Mr. Barrington?"

"What? Who are you?"

He jerked up and fumbled for his glasses. Professor Hellman was right. Charlie was afraid of something.

I reintroduced myself and reminded him that we had met once before.

"Oh, yeah. That's right. The girl detective. I remember." He reached for the electric controls and raised the head of his bed. "Sit down. Did you know Joan's dead?"

"Yes, sir. I know. I found her."

I pulled the green armchair around so that I could face him and sat.

"Oh, yeah, I think somebody told me that." He nodded several times, trying to put it all together. "Did you find out who killed Lois?"

"Not yet. I'm still hoping you can help me."

"I can't pay you, you know that. I'm broke. Do you work for free?"

"No. Professor Hellman is paying me."

Charlie smiled, with a delight that made me uncomfortable.

"Him? He's paying you? Didn't think he had it in him to do anything about anything."

"I don't think you're being fair to him."

"Probably not. Nobody ever said I was fair. Don't like him much, never did. But I guess he was good enough to Lois. Or maybe he thinks they'll be after him next."

"Who?"

He shut his mouth and glared at me.

"Whoever. I don't know. That's what you're supposed to find out."

I glared back.

"Charlie, how can I help you if you won't tell me what's going on?"

"Maybe nothin's goin' on. Maybe Joan killed Lois and then herself."

He clicked on the television set. A local anchor who owed his livelihood to his dentist and his hairdresser was doing his best imitation of big-city news.

"Wanta watch the news with me? This guy's good—as good as Dan Rather. He did a report on water rights—made me glad I don't have any land to worry about. There's advantages to being poor, you know."

"I'm afraid I can't see them. Look, if somebody is really killing members of your family, and you're afraid they're after you, don't you think you should talk about it? Do you really think you're safe in here?"

His face sagged.

"No, I don't think that at all. Jesus may help me, but talking won't."

"Please, Charlie."

He clicked the remote and the sound from an ad for a carpet store almost knocked me out of the room. Begging wasn't going to do it, and I don't get a kick out of terrorizing old men. I left.

Mrs. Schueller was still on the phone. I got out with only another wave.

"You did what?" Deke asked, closing his red-rimmed eyes in pain.

I had decided I could think better on a full stomach, and had discovered Deke at the counter of the Mother Lode coffee shop, already cutting his steak. I quickly and randomly marked my Keno ticket and waved it at the runner before I answered.

"I sent Mick's check back. And I went to see Charlie. And I'm not sure what my next step is. I'll try Julie Barrington again, and I have a new address for Stephanie Johnson—I haven't staked it out for Mary Yates because I thought I was off the case. And then there's Irene Rebideaux. Martinez. I might learn something if I tailed her for a few days. I still think Castle Properties is involved in this somehow."

My hamburger arrived, and I dumped ketchup on my fries.

"Okay," he sighed.

"Okay what? I told you there was no money in this."

"Okay I'll take the Stephanie Johnson side. Ain't no way she gonna talk to you. Particularly after you been around asking questions of Aunt Mae. If she talks to me, might save you a few days of sitting around waiting."

"You don't have to do this, you know. I didn't ask for help."

"Yeah, I know. You didn't ask for help and you don't need it. And maybe I ain't gonna give it. But I'll see what I can do with Stephanie Johnson."

"Okay. Thanks."

The Keno board lit up. I lost again. Deke finished his steak and left. I had a cup of coffee that was sure to keep me awake and played three more Keno tickets before I gave up and went home.

The coffee didn't exactly keep me awake, but I didn't sleep well. Butch decided that whatever was going on, he needed his sleep, and moved to a chair. Sundance remained faithful, rearranging himself and going right back to sleep whenever I thrashed. And I can't even blame the coffee for my restlessness. There were two thoughts running around in my head, and either one of them could have destroyed a night's sleep.

The first was about Lucas Hecht. I wanted to see him again. He seemed to be a nice guy, and I don't run into many nice guys, and I wanted to see him again. More than that, I wanted to sleep with him again. On the other hand, I don't have a very good record as far as relationships are concerned. And I had decided a couple of years earlier that two strikes were enough, that maybe I was better off just making it on my own, and forgetting the whole idea of having a man in my life, except for Deke, which God knows was not a romantic relationship. And now here I was, thinking about somebody I should probably just write off as a one-night stand.

Besides, he lived in Las Vegas—Echo Bay, which was worse. How could I have a relationship with somebody who lived 450 miles away, when I couldn't make one work in the same town? I had a reason to go to Las Vegas maybe once a year, and Lucas didn't seem the type who would have much call to come to Reno. Still, every time I tried to push him down to the bottom of my mind, he popped right back up.

The other thought was about Mick. I didn't want Mick to be involved in something wrong, I really didn't. And I didn't have any hard evidence to implicate him. On the other hand, he tried twice to buy me off. And $5000 sure seemed like overkill to me. I would have felt better if he had shown a little grief, over his wife, if not his sister-in-law. He had looked strained, but not grieving. Like a worried man, not a sad one. I could do a credit check fairly easily—at least find out if $5000 was a lot of money to Mick—and maybe Rudy Stapp could let me know where Mick works, what he does. I would have to pay Rudy full salary, even though I was working for less, but it would be cheaper than going back to Las Vegas and following Mick to work myself. Anyway, Mick might spot me if I tried to tail him.

I got up and sent a message by modem. Rudy would get

it whenever he checked his computer. I hoped taking action would help me sleep, but it didn't. I kept thinking how easy it would be for Mick, the ex-lifeguard, to swim to the houseboat and back. And I didn't like it. Besides, why would he do it?

With some relief I discovered a third thought trying to break through: Charlie and his fear. Charlie wouldn't be afraid of Mick, or at least if it were that simple, he would tell somebody. Maybe not me, but somebody.

I fell asleep at dawn, of course, so by the time I woke again the sun was filtering through my window shades. I lost my grip as I was raising one of the shades, and it snapped up to the top, setting loose a cloud of dust from the cheap open-weave cotton curtains I had hung when I moved in, always intending to replace them. I thought about taking them off the rods right then and dropping them in a heap next to my laundry hamper, so I could take them to the laundromat at some point. But I didn't know when that would be, so I left them up. I could do something about the house when I had finished the case.

By the time I had showered and put on a clean blue shirt and a clean pair of jeans, it was late enough that I could drive over to see if Julie Barrington was home. I thought about calling first, but I find that sometimes I do better with people when they aren't expecting me, and they haven't had time to prepare a face.

The Blazer was in the driveway, the Cougar wasn't. I hoped that meant Julie was there alone. I just wasn't looking forward to coping with her model again.

She opened the door in her bathrobe, a dirty purple terry-cloth float that zipped up the front. She brushed her hair out of her face with the hand that wasn't holding the cigarette. Her eyes were stark and sunken.

"Come on in," she said with a shrug. Once again, she turned away and walked down the hall, leaving me to shut the door and follow.

This time she led me only as far as a room to the left of

the entrance. It was a living room of sorts—unlike her studio, it didn't really look as if anyone lived there. The rough wood and pillow furniture had come out of a Santa Fe-style decorator's shop, and just about the only personal touch was a large painting, an abstract done mostly in the same pink and sand as the pastel pillow covers. There was a sense of humor, self-mockery, in the painting, and I wished I could have asked her about it. Maybe another time.

She stood, her back to me, staring out the window at the rolling green vista and the purple hills, a freshly lit cigarette in her hand. A large pink ashtray on one of several small tables was overflowing with butts. The room stank.

I stood, too. I had thought this time couldn't be worse than the first time, but I wasn't prepared for the change in her. Somebody once described the difference between the original and the copy as the energy of the artist. I was looking at the copy, the Portrait of the Artist as an Old Woman, energy removed.

Finally she turned.

"What do you want from me?"

"I want you to help me find out who killed your daughters."

She shook her head.

"Joan committed suicide. They told me Joan committed suicide."

Not even accidental overdose.

"What do you think?"

"What the hell does it matter what I think? I think I'm old and tired and they were taken away from me years ago. They weren't mine, they were his. He made them his. So he has lost his daughters. His daughters are dead. That's what I think."

"But you could help me do something about it."

"No. There's nothing to be done."

"Don't you worry, at all, that whoever killed them might be after you next?"

That was a low shot, but it was the only one I could think of.

Something gurgled in her throat that wasn't a laugh.

"They had no connection with me. Someone might be after him, killing them might be someone's idea of slow torture, and I could understand that, if I hadn't known them once, if I hadn't remembered when they were once my daughters, I might have felt that way, too. Certainly, there was a time I would have killed him. But no one would care if I died. I wouldn't care if I died."

The cigarette was about to burn her fingers. I walked over and took it from her, burrowing into the ashtray until I found a spot hard enough to put it out.

"Who would hate Charlie that much?"

"Who wouldn't?"

"Please tell me about it, tell me whatever you can."

I hated this. I'm just not comfortable with this kind of emotion, and I couldn't decide whether she had been in shock the first time I saw her or was in shock now. I took her hands and led her to a chaise. She sat.

"Is there something I can get you? Tea? Coffee?"

She thought.

"Tea, thank you. I could use a cup of tea."

I headed in the direction where I thought I could find the kitchen. I felt funny fixing her tea in her own house. The kitchen was at the back of the house, the left turn where the right turn was the hall to the studio. It was a large room, the kind of kitchen that belonged in a ranch-style house, complete with butcher-block counter in the middle. The stove and refrigerator and sink all appeared to be the original white models, no updates here. The cabinets had been painted white several years before, and nobody had wiped the fingerprints off in a while. Some dirty cups sat in the sink.

I ran water into a battered copper teakettle and turned on the burner. Then I tried cupboards, looking for clean cups and teabags. Not much there. Julie Barrington evidently didn't like to cook any more than I did. I found teabags—Earl Grey—in a bamboo container and rinsed out two pottery mugs. I hoped she didn't want anything in her tea.

She didn't. She accepted the mug I handed her gratefully, dipped the bag a couple of times, and dropped it in the ashtray. I let mine steep a little longer and did the same. Tea oozed out among the cigarette butts.

"Julie," I began.

My voice startled her. I had to reach to steady her mug.

"I'm sorry. If you want me to leave, I will."

She shook her head.

"It doesn't matter. It doesn't matter anymore."

"Something has to matter, dammit. Please, please, just let me ask you about a couple of things."

She shrugged.

"Okay. The last time I was here, you said you would understand if somebody had killed Joan. What did you mean?"

"Oh, hell, nothing. Joan was a pain in the ass, that's all, never thought about anybody but herself, just like Charlie."

"That's all?"

"That's all."

"Do you know how Mary Yates was picked to look after Charlie?"

She shook her head.

"Was it Lois who found her?"

She shrugged.

"Well—do you know anything about a company called Castle Properties? Any connection Charlie might have had with them?"

"What?"

"I just keep thinking this whole thing about drugs isn't it. There has to be something else. And it seems to always come back to Castle Properties. I wondered if Charlie was connected with them."

"Oh, my God, how would I know?"

"Well, you might, if it was a long time ago. Or you might

know who to send me to, who might be able to tell me something.''

"If it was an investment, John Woodruff might know.''

"John Woodruff?''

"He used to handle everything for us, and even after the divorce he still handled everything. The financial crap was too complicated for us to ever really disentangle. Johnny retired a few years ago. Van's his son. Van took over when Johnny retired. He might know. Why do you want to know about an investment?''

"I don't know. I wish I did.''

I finished my tea and said good-bye. I reached Carson City before I had time to do anything but frown.

The blue Mercedes was in the parking lot when I drove by. I hadn't remembered to bring something to read, and I didn't know how long I'd have to wait, so I turned back to the main drag and stopped at a drugstore. I hate buying paperbacks in drugstores. All they ever have are mysteries and romances. I grabbed a *Harper*'s—I could do the crostic puzzle while I waited.

I drove back to the small office building. The Mercedes was gone.

I read the magazine and then just sat for the rest of the afternoon. But I had blown the day—the Mercedes didn't come back. I had a feeling this was becoming a very expensive case.

Chapter
8

DEKE WASN'T AT the Mother Lode counter, where I had hoped to find him. I ate my hamburger alone, played a couple of Keno tickets, and it was still only eight o'clock. I was feeling restless, so I started walking, away from the neon, past the Twilight Zone of the Midnight Mission, shaking my head at the unshaven bum in his ratty overcoat who called out, "Hey, Princess, take me home with you," and four blocks later I found myself back in civilization, walking up the steps of the Reno Theatrical Society.

The narrow lobby, dominated by the long counter, like a saloon, was empty. The walls were liver-colored, with sconces, adding to the saloon feeling. The doors to the auditorium were closed. I slipped through them into the dark and felt my way to an empty aisle seat.

Van Woodruff was on the stage talking in a loud fake voice to some woman I didn't know. I must have walked in on a dress rehearsal, because he was wearing a minister's reverse-collar shirt beneath a tweed sports jacket. The woman was wearing tight pants, a metallic sweater, and long earrings, Reno's idea of what actresses look like. She answered in a similarly loud fake voice. Then there was a long silence.

"Oh, *hell*," Van shouted. "Where the hell is Lurene? What's so damned difficult about this entrance that she just can't seem to make it on time?"

"All right, everybody, calm down," said a voice from an unseen source in the audience. I don't know who "everybody" was supposed to be. Only Van seemed upset. "Lurene?" the voice continued, louder. "Lurene? Where are you, honey? Eddie, is Lurene backstage?"

A young guy in jeans and a sweatshirt came out on stage.

"She's on her way up from the dressing room," he said, gesturing vaguely with his clipboard.

"Oh, *hell*," Van shouted again. He marched to a sofa and sat down with such emphasis that the set shook.

After some thirty seconds of total silence, Lurene poked her head around the corner of the set.

"I'm sorry," she said. "I really am. But it's such a quick change, and I just don't seem to be able to make it in time."

"Quick change!" Van was back on his feet. "There's an act break! How the hell can it be a quick change when there's an act break!"

"All right, all right," said the voice from the audience. "Let's take it from the top of the scene. And tomorrow night, Eddie, make sure that Lurene is ready before we start."

Everyone left the stage, and a phone started ringing. The woman in the metallic sweater dashed on to answer it. Van entered, she hung up, and they started talking in the loud fake voices again. This time Lurene made her entrance. She looked pretty on stage. Whoever had helped her with makeup had changed her totally. I hoped she could hold on to the change, carry it away with her when the play was over.

As close as I could figure out the plot, the actress was looking for something that the vicar wasn't supposed to know she had, and Lurene had found it but didn't know what it was. The play probably would have been funnier if I had seen it from the beginning. And the stops and starts and backups to get the light and sound cues right didn't help.

I didn't see the end, either, because about quarter to eleven the voice in the audience called, "Okay, that's it for tonight. We'll start Act Three tomorrow night at seven o'clock sharp.''

"For God's sake, Bud, when are we going to run this thing from beginning to end," Van exploded from the stage. "We open next week and we haven't had a run-through yet!"

"Don't worry, it'll come together. Once we get the pieces right, you'll be amazed at the way it'll all come together."

Van stalked off the stage, apparently unconvinced.

The houselights came up. I was the only person in the audience except for Bud Herrick, owner of Herrick Insurance by day and artistic director of the Reno Theatrical Society by night. I hadn't seen him in years—not since he came to see his daughter Sandra in a play at UNR, and I happened to be there the same night—and actually I didn't know him, I only knew who he was. I was surprised at the whiteness of his hair and the redness of his face.

He turned and saw me.

"Hi, there. Waiting for someone?"

"Sort of, Mr. Herrick. I was hoping I could catch Van Woodruff for a minute."

"Well, you might want to wait outside. I'm going to be closing up the theater now, and Van usually leaves by the stage door."

He gave me a genial smile, without recognition. I thanked him and left.

The night was cool, and I was sorry I had a long walk home ahead of me. I started to shiver, standing in the parking lot, with nothing between me and the chill air but a denim jacket. Nights like that used to be clear—you could look up and see a sky full of stars. I looked up and saw the pale gray haze of neon reflecting from a low smog cover.

People began filing out of the stage door. The woman who played the actress, now in jeans and a heavy coat. The young man without his clipboard. I heard bits of conversation, centering on who was going for coffee. Van Woodruff was one of the last.

"Mr. Woodruff!" I called.

He was surprised to see me, but at least he recognized me. It was a good thing I wasn't hoping for a smile, because I didn't get one.

"What is it?" he asked sharply.

"I'm sorry to bother you at the theater, sir, but it seemed the easiest way to catch you." He didn't react, so I continued. "I'm trying to find out what the connection is between Charlie Barrington and Castle Properties, and I thought you might be able to help me."

He blinked, and I thought there was something going on inside him, but I couldn't read it.

"I have no idea what you're talking about." His voice was quiet, controlled. "And now that your client is dead, it seems to me that you have no legitimate interest in the Barrington family."

"Well, I have a new client, Mr. Woodruff, so my interest is legitimate."

"Who?"

"You know I can't tell you that."

He nodded. He was staring at me, and I didn't want to look away. He still had some makeup left around his eyes, and his hair was ruffled, right above his ears. He looked like an owl, an angry owl. I didn't see him as handsome anymore.

"So anyway," I continued, "it seems to me that whatever is going on with the Barringtons has something to do with Castle Properties. And I hoped you might help me find out what the connection is. Mrs. Barrington—Julie—thought it might have been some investment made when your father was in charge."

"A little research would tell you that Charlie went through a bankruptcy—because of his own bad business decisions. Any investments made when my father was in charge were wiped out then, along with everything else."

"Then you can't help me with Castle Properties?"

"I can't."

"Is there some way I could talk to your father?"

This time he smiled, and I wished that he hadn't.

"You could, but I don't think it will help you. My father is in a room down the hall from Charlie Barrington. He has Alzheimer's. He doesn't remember anything, not even who he is."

"I'm sorry."

"So am I. Good night, Miss O'Neal."

He got into a black 911 Porsche, slammed it into gear, and roared off down Sierra Street. I followed on foot, getting colder by the minute.

I had gone about half a block when a horn beeped and someone called, "I remember you. Do you need a ride?"

It was Lurene, in a green VW Rabbit. I accepted.

"You're the detective who asked about the woman who murdered her sister," she said.

"Something like that," I answered, still shivering. The car's heater was humming, but only cold air was flowing onto my feet.

"What were you doing at the rehearsal?"

"Still looking for answers to some questions."

She nodded.

"Which way?"

I gave her directions.

"So what have you found out? Did she do it?"

"I don't think so. She's dead now, too."

Lurene looked puzzled. She still had her stage makeup on, strengthening her dark blue eyes, her blond hair was curling softly over the collar of her sheepskin jacket, and I hoped she had somewhere to go, someone to meet, looking that pretty.

"Why would she be dead?"

"Well, I don't know. The police are calling it an accidental overdose, but not everyone believes it. That's why I was asking questions."

"Of Van. You were asking Van questions."

"Yes, I was."

"You think he had something to do with it."

"I don't know that. I was hoping he could help me get some information I need."

"Oh."

I let the silence hold for a couple of blocks.

"Do you know Van well?"

"Not really. We've kind of become friends since we've been doing the play together. You know."

I thought about Van Woodruff yelling at her missed entrance. I wondered what kind of a friend he would be.

"Has he ever mentioned the Barringtons to you?"

"No. Why would he?"

She concentrated on her driving.

"I thought he might, you know, since Joan Halliday had been his client, and since it would have been important to the case if you had been able to either confirm or deny Joan's presence at the airport the day her sister was murdered."

"Oh. But it doesn't matter now, does it, now that she's dead?"

"Well, it might matter more, if the same person killed both of them."

It was like talking to a child, even though Lurene was probably within a couple of years of my age. Someone who either wouldn't or couldn't make connections. I wanted to know what she knew, what Van had told her. I also wanted to be careful of her, because I sensed there would be a blow coming, and I didn't want to be the one to deliver it. Whatever Van was doing with Lurene, it was for his own purposes, and it wasn't going to do her any good.

As we turned onto High Street, I thanked her for the ride.

"I hope I haven't made you too late to join the others for coffee," I said.

"No, it's okay. I wasn't going to meet the others anyway." She hesitated, started to add something else, then said, "You're welcome for the ride. You lead such an exciting life—it's fun talking to you."

I don't see my life as exciting, and I didn't want to think what her life must be like to imagine mine that way.

I said good night and walked up onto the porch, but as she drove off I dashed to the Mustang. I had to see if I was right.

I followed the Rabbit back along Mill Street to Virginia, then south several blocks. The car slowed, then turned into the driveway of a small motel. I slowed just enough to watch Lurene park the car, right next to a black 911 Porsche. I noted the name on the motel—Sleepy Hollow— because I knew I would have to check the owner. And I was betting that, one more time, it would be Castle Properties Inc.

When I got home, I was greeted by two hungry cats and a blinking light on my answering machine. I took care of the cats first, then checked the single message. Lucas Hecht. Just wanted to make sure I was all right.

Sometimes when I can't sleep I lie in bed very quietly, listening to Butch snore, and I try to decide whether it would be better or worse if someone—some man—was lying there snoring, not just a fat gray cat. And I can't. There's no simple answer. Partly because I can't decide what I would want from him, if he was lying there snoring and I was awake. Would I want him to sleep through my insomnia? Would I want him to wake up and ask what was wrong? Suppose I said nothing was wrong? Would I want him to turn over and go back to sleep? Or would I want more concern than that? What would I want?

I don't even know how to think about what he might want from me.

When I'm thoroughly frantic, I ease my way out of bed and stretch, first holding on to the doorjamb and pulling, then bending over and bouncing my palms against the floor, trying to dissipate the tension in my body without disturbing the cats. When my nerve endings quit spitting anxiety, I slide back into the narrow channel they've left for me, arranging the angles of my body around their curves.

Making the question specific, asking if I wanted Lucas Hecht there, that night, didn't help me find an answer. I just didn't know. When I thought about his body, the answer was yes. When I thought about waking up in the morning and actually having to deal with another human being, any human being, I got scared. I didn't know how that would work. It sure hadn't with my parents, and I think there was a time when they loved each other a lot. So I didn't sleep too well, and I was glad one more time to see the dawn, so I could get some rest.

And then I actually called Lucas Hecht first thing in the morning—more or less. I didn't think I was going to do that, but after I washed and brushed and fixed a cup of instant coffee, I remembered the boiled coffee in the blue enamel pot at the houseboat, and I called him.

He answered at the shop—it was the same phone number, store and houseboat. His voice changed when I told him who it was.

"I wasn't sure you'd call," he said.

"Yeah, well, I wasn't sure I would, either."

"Tom told me that Joan Halliday's death was quickly and officially ruled an accidental overdose. Is that okay with you?"

"No. No, it isn't."

"Does that mean you're still investigating?"

"Yeah, I have a new client paying me to stick with it."

"Good—if it means you have to come back to Echo Bay. I'd like to see you again."

My heart stopped and started a couple of times, and when I was sure I could control my voice, I said, "Probably I will have to come down there. I'm not sure. I could call you, when I know."

"I'd like that. I hope it's soon."

"Okay—I'll call you."

That was the best I could do. I hung up the phone and fixed another cup of instant coffee.

I know other people have been devastated by lousy relationships. This is not unique to me, and I know that. And I can't say with either of them—the great love of my life or the rebound almost-great love of my life—that they were lousy human beings, or that I made bad choices. The relationships just didn't work. That's what they said, both times. And since both of them are happily married to other people—and even my mother seems to be doing okay the second time around—I have to figure it's me. Since it's me, the odds aren't very good that I'm going to do any better with somebody new.

I thought about flying down to Las Vegas, driving to Echo Bay, looking Lucas Hecht straight in the eye, and telling him I didn't want to start anything because I knew it wouldn't work.

I thought about him smiling, and putting his arms around me. I thought about the fresh smell of his body, the deceptive hardness, muscles beneath flesh beneath rough skin, and I wasn't sure what I would say when I saw him. When I saw him. I shivered a little. I was going to see him again.

Only a soft gray light was filtering into my office, so I was startled when I turned on my computer and the time check informed me it was almost noon. I had wasted half the damn day thinking about a man.

I had a message from Rudy Stapp. Mick had no VMS—that's visible means of support. But he lived well, seemed from his spotty credit record to alternate feast and famine, months of slow pay were ended by a sudden influx of cash. When he had to list an occupation, it was professional gambler. Stapp had also talked to Sgt. Morrison, and had one piece of information to add: There was some kind of pressure, Morrison wouldn't say from where, to take care of "things"—meaning Joan Halliday's body—quickly and quietly. Invoice will follow, the message ended. Right. And I was going to end up working for free.

Handling this myself—no more Rudy Stapp—what should I do next? What would happen if I talked to Mick—if I just laid it all out for him and asked him for an explanation? Best case, he'd give me one. Worst case, I'd be in trouble.

Either case meant Las Vegas, which brought me full circle to Lucas Hecht. But I wasn't going to waste any more time on that. I was going back to Carson, to Irene Rebideaux Martinez and Castle Properties, this time armed with *Newsweek* and *Atlantic Monthly*.

My timing was off again. As I was slowing down, where 395 hit the Carson City city limits, I saw a black 911 Porsche speeding up, going the other way. While I couldn't have picked the driver out of a lineup, I was pretty certain he was Van Woodruff. There was no point in following him back to Reno. But I sure wished I knew where he had been in Carson.

I drove-thru a fast-food joint and settled in across the street from the low stone office building with a hamburger, fried zucchini, and a Coke. I had checked to make sure that the blue Mercedes was in the lot and then parked far enough away that I could just see the exit. I didn't know how often I would have to come back, and I didn't want Irene spotting my car.

I took one break to stretch my legs and find a public rest room—no small trick since gas stations have quit being service stations. This may be the only real contribution of casinos to our society. The last remaining public johns.

This time, I didn't miss Irene. She left the building a little after five, and a few minutes later I saw her car turn left out of the parking lot and then south on 395. When she turned right onto King's Canyon Road, I dropped back a little farther than I wanted to. I was about halfway to the junction with 50 when I was certain she wasn't ahead of me any longer. I turned back, trying to decide where I had lost her. I couldn't be sure, but I was willing to bet it was at a turnoff marked Private Drive—No Trespassing. I checked the mileage back to 395, so that I could find the area on an assessor's map. I was starting to feel nuts. What was it going to prove, even if I discovered that Castle Properties owned half the state?

I kept trying to imagine the connections on the drive back to Reno, but sequence was still raveling out of reach like balls across the floor, as Emily Dickinson would put it. Or dice across the table, maybe. Part of the problem was that I just didn't know what the game was, if it wasn't drugs. I wasn't sure what the game was even if it *was* drugs.

Deke was at his spot at the Mother Lode counter when I

arrived. He nodded as I sat down next to him. He didn't smile. I wondered sometimes what his round cheeks and sagging jowls would look like if he smiled, but I suspected I would never find out. At first I had thought he never smiled at me because he didn't like me. At the time I thought he had reason not to like me—I had met Deke when I was trying to find a friend of his who had run up a lot of bills on the woman he was living with and then split. Deke showed up in my office one day with the guy and the money. A couple of weeks later, he sat down next to me at the Mother Lode counter one night. Then we just got into the habit of having dinner together. Not every night, but usually a couple of times a week. After several months of this, I realized that I shouldn't take his dour outlook personally. So I try not to.

He had ordered before I arrived, so when Diane brought his steak I asked for a club sandwich and beer.

"What's with you?" he asked. "You always order a hamburger."

"I had one for lunch. I can't handle more than one a day."

I told him what had happened the last couple of days, except I left out Lucas Hecht's phone call. I hadn't told Deke what had happened with Lucas in Echo Bay because I didn't figure it was any of his business.

"So you think this Mick Halliday is going to tell you the truth just because he taught you to swim and you thought he was cute when you was eight?"

"He might. Particularly if the truth is something simple and he doesn't have anything to do with either of the murders or what Charlie is afraid of. Charlie wouldn't be afraid of Mick, I'm sure of that."

"But you think Mick might know just what Charlie is afraid of—and that he'll just up and tell you?"

"You think I'm dumb, I know."

"Not dumb. I just think you go running off without thinking things through sometimes."

"Okay. I'll think it through before I go talk to Mick."
Deke glared, but didn't stop chewing.

"What happened with Stephanie Johnson?"

"I met her."

"And?"

"That little three-year-old, Brian, he ran right out into the
street and I almost hit him. I was driving the truck, too, and
he would have been squashed flat. I took him back to his
mama and gave her a piece of my mind."

"Really? That was a stroke of luck."

"It was a stroke of luck I didn't kill that child. His mama
ain't much more than a girl, and she ain't looking after him
right. I told her so, too."

"What'd she say?"

"She started crying, then she stopped and asked would I
like a beer or something. So I said yes, and asked her why
she wasn't doing a better job with her kids. She said ain't
nobody to help her with them, Todd's daddy run off to LA
and she don't know where Brian's daddy is, and sometimes
she just gets tired. I tell her I know. I asked her about her
mama, why she don't help. She tell me her mama used to
help, but she moved to Las Vegas, where her aunt is. So I
told her I'd take the kids Saturday afternoon, take 'em over
to Idlewild to feed the ducks, or something."

"You did *what*?"

"I just told you what I did."

"And she's just letting you take her kids? Deke, you
could be a child molester or something!"

"Yeah, but I ain't. And that way she can get her hair
done."

"Why does she want to get her hair done?"

"Why not? Don't you ever get your hair done? No, don't
answer, all I have to do is look at you to know you don't."

I cringed.

"That's not fair. I get my hair done sometimes."

"When? When you ever get your hair done?"

"I get it cut a couple of times a year."

"Yeah, but you don't get it *done*. You just have some damn *unisex* barber whack it off more or less even, as if you don't care what you look like, as if you don't ever want some man to look at you and think you look good."

"I don't look that bad."

"You *do*. Your fingernails are all torn up and you don't wear lipstick and you do look that bad."

I almost shot back by telling him about Lucas. But I was afraid he was right, that I did look that bad. Maybe Lucas had never really gotten a good look at me.

"Why are you saying this? I thought you liked me the way I am."

"I do. I'm just afraid nobody else will, and it ain't gonna do you no good to spend all the evenings for the rest of your life hanging out with a black man old enough to be your daddy."

"I never thought of you that way—I just thought of you as my friend."

"I am your friend, and about your only friend, too. How come you ain't got no girlfriends?"

"I don't know—I guess I never wanted any."

Deke snorted. I hadn't ever seen anyone snort before, but that's what he did. Through his nose, like a horse.

I looked at the last quarter of my club sandwich, and I didn't want it. I waved to Diane to get me another beer and reached for a Keno ticket.

"So. You're going to take the two little boys to Idlewild Saturday to feed the ducks while Stephanie gets her hair done, which she is going to do just because she feels like it, and not because she wants to look good for some man."

"Or maybe she wants to look good for me."

"You?"

"I told her when I brought the kids back, I'd bring in some Chinese for dinner."

"Jesus, Deke, if I'm young enough to be your daughter, what's she?"

"None of your business, that's what she is."

"And how is she going to feel when she discovers the only reason you're doing this is to find out about her mother and Willie Carver and Charlie Barrington?"

"Maybe that's the only reason, maybe it ain't. I'll tell you what I find out about her mama, because I said I would. But that don't mean I can't have other interests here, that I can tell you about or not, as I choose. Stephanie Johnson didn't do nothing wrong except maybe love the wrong men a couple of times and not take good enough care of herself when they left her. And you got no call to be sitting there passing judgments."

I watched the Keno board light up. I lost.

"Okay. I guess you're right. I'm sorry. Let me know what you want to let me know."

I grabbed my check and left.

I couldn't help looking at my hands, though, as I gave the check and the money to the cashier. Deke was right. My nails were all torn up. Sometimes I just filed them off flat, but I hadn't even done that in a while.

As I rode down the escalator into the casino, I looked at the women around me. I thought how I'd look with styled hair, and makeup, and a manicure, and a sweatshirt cat with jeweled eyes. Probably I'd look like a tall, raw-boned woman who was all dressed up with no place to go.

At the bottom of the escalator I almost ran into a twenty-one dealer with layered honey-blond hair that waved around her face and shoulders.

"Excuse me. Where do you get your hair done?"

"The Flamingo Hilton. Ask for Barry," she said as she got on the escalator.

I figured I could think about that in the morning.

Chapter
9

I WENT TO sleep smarting from what Deke had said, and I woke up the same way. I don't think of myself as unattractive. I do think of myself as plain. My eyes are sort of an interesting color—hazel is what my driver's license says—and my nose is straight, but I have freckles, and my chin is best described as stubborn. When I was a kid, well-meaning adults would tell me I had pretty hair. Or exclaim about how smart I was, or—worst of all—how big for my age. So I never tried for glamour. Instead, I have opted for a low-maintenance way of life. That means I don't do anything more with my face than wash it, and I don't do anything more with my hair than wash it, brush it, and catch it with an elastic band. My clothes fit right in—a lot of cotton and denim, stuff that goes into a washer and dryer. I have a suit for the rare occasions when I testify in court. If I'm clean, I'm presentable. That ought to be enough. If Deke didn't think so, that was his problem.

What bothered me more than his comment about my looks was his accusation that I was almost friendless. I do have friends, sort of, but most of them are like Terry Dickerson, professional relationships. Not people I hang out with, just to have a good time. I'm not sure just how that happened, when I grew up and went all the way through school in Reno, that everybody but me had close friends. I think it may have happened when I skipped fifth grade. If not then, it was in high school. I was tall and awkward and shy and I didn't join anything except the National Honor Society, and that was only because they asked. I always envied the kids who had friends, the ones who went to football games and proms, who all went out for pizza together.

Somehow that gave me an idea that I wasn't very proud of, because I managed to go from "friends" to "high school" to "who could help me with this case."

Sandra Herrick, once a cheerleader for the Reno High football team and then the star of the UNR Theater Department, had become a reporter for the Nevada *Herald*. I had never developed a good source at the newspaper, and this might be a good moment to try again. Sandra had been a year ahead of me in high school, but we had been in Professor Hellman's Western Civ course together, and she would no doubt be curious about the Barrington story. A little information trade seemed possible.

I called, she remembered me, and she was free for lunch. I was just as happy to put off Carson and Irene for another day. Sandra suggested Harrah's at noon. I agreed—it would be a change from the Mother Lode.

Sandra was ten minutes late, and as I watched her entrance, I began to rethink Deke's gibes and the possibility of calling Barry at the Flamingo Hilton. She was wearing a blue paisley dress with a high neck and draped skirt, a blue jacket, gold necklace and earrings, and she managed to look professional, feminine, and casual, all at the same time. Whoever cut her frosted hair wasn't into unisex, her nails were natural but glossy, and she was wearing more makeup than just lipstick—carefully applied, of course.

By the time I was fifteen, I was a good six inches taller than my mother. Walking down the street with her, I would begin to imagine myself growing larger and larger, like Alice eating the wrong side of the mushroom, until I was certain that everyone for blocks around was staring at the giantess lumbering along next to the petite, fashionable woman, who took tiny high-heeled steps.

"Stand up straight!" my mother would snap. "Be proud of your height!"

I tried, but there was so much to be proud of. Now, it doesn't bother me so much, and I do stand up straight, but I still get uncomfortable when I think people might be looking at me. All eyes followed Sandra to the table, and I was certain the minds behind them wondered what that stunning woman was doing lunching with the country mouse. Make that country horse. Sandra didn't seem to notice.

"So, Freddie," she said as she slipped into the booth, "good to see you. What have you been doing for the last ten years?"

"I'm a PI—private investigator. For the last five years, anyway."

I handed a Keno ticket to the runner. I had already lost twice while I was waiting for Sandra.

When I looked at her again, she was sitting there smiling brightly, obviously waiting for me to continue. Telling Professor Hellman why I was a PI was one thing. Telling her was something else again.

"What about you? What have you been doing?"

"I spent two years with KRNO, married Don Echeverria—remember him?—was hassled by the station management when I got pregnant, decided reading news to a camera was no way for an adult to earn a living anyway, quit and went to work for the *Herald*. Now I write news."

"Oh. I had wondered why you left television—you were really good."

"Thanks. I may go back, as a matter of fact. If they'll let me cover Carson and do political commentary."

"Hey, that sounds like a good deal."

A waitress walked up and stood next to the table, pencil poised over her pad, daring us to ignore her and continue our conversation. We didn't. Sandra ordered a chef's salad,

I ordered the same. I wanted to see how change felt, and I thought I might do it a little at a time.

The waitress left, and Sandra was still smiling.

"I guess you're wondering why I called," I said.

"Of course, I want all the details. I gather it's business. And of course I'm curious what your case is and what you think I might know."

"Well—there is a case, and I do want to talk to you about it, but I could have come to your office to do that. I really thought it would be nice to have lunch."

Her smile was still bright, but not as brittle around the edges.

"Welcome to the new girl network," she said.

"Thanks." This time I felt like smiling back. "I need to find out whatever I can about Castle Properties."

"Who are they and why do you need to find out about them?"

I didn't tell her about Lucas Hecht, or Deke, or Stephanie Johnson, or that Professor Hellman had hired me. But I told her about Joan Halliday, and that I kept running into Castle Properties wherever I turned. I talked through the salads and into coffee. She kept nodding.

"Interesting," she finally said.

"Well? What can you tell me?"

"I don't know. I don't know anything about Castle Properties—I've never heard of them, in fact. But Hank d'Arbanville is a major client of Don's law firm—he's with Woodruff, Wallace, Manoukian and Lagomarsino—so I may be able to find out something. I know Hank's ambitious, and he has a lot staked on his run for the Senate next year. And since he's running against an incumbent, it's going to be expensive. Even though the incumbent is following in the great tradition of second-rate Nevada senators."

"What about Joaquin Meara?"

"I know him only by reputation. He's supposed to have been a buddy of Charlie Barrington's in the Last Good War, and then a silent partner in the Mother Lode—silent because he's rumored to have had connections to organized crime.''

''That sounds like we're connecting Hank d'Arbanville to organized crime.''

''We might be. But we need more to go on. Oh, this is exciting!'' She wriggled in her seat like a kid. ''How about lunch on Monday?''

''Make it Tuesday. I think I may fly to Vegas for the weekend.''

''I'll see you then.''

Since Sandra was checking out Castle Properties and maybe Joaquin Meara, and Deke was following up on Stephanie Johnson, Las Vegas was certainly the place I could be most effective. I could talk to Mick, I could hit Aunt Mae's place again (or at least drive by). And then there was the shrink Joan had been seeing. Shrinks won't normally tell you much, but maybe with Joan dead—if he didn't think she was suicidal—I might get something out of him. I called Lucas Hecht when I got home.

''It looks like I have to come down this weekend,'' I told him, ''so I thought I'd see if you were going to be around.''

''Yes, I'll be here. No plans. That's great, really great. When are you going to get here?''

''I'll fly down Friday. It'll probably be late before I get out to Echo Bay, though.''

''What about dinner? Will you be here in time for dinner?''

''Well, yeah, I guess I could be. Sure.''

I felt unsteady the whole time I talked to him and terrified when I hung up the phone. What if I got down there and we didn't like each other? What if he looked at me and decided he'd made a terrible mistake? I could shake his hand and leave, that's what I'd have to do.

The Flamingo Hilton Beauty Salon was listed, and Barry could see me Thursday afternoon at three. I almost asked about a manicure, but that was more than I could handle. I would see how I felt about my hair first. And what happened in Las Vegas.

This—right here—is the big hangup in sexual politics. I had just met this man (okay, and just slept with him) and I was already trying to figure out how much or how little I was willing to change so he would find me attractive, so that maybe this one would last for a while. Not that having something done with my hair should be that big a deal. Some women have their hair done and their nails done just because it's the way they like to look. But I've never been into that—I suppose it felt too much like competing with my mother, and that was impossible—so it was looming large.

And if I got my hair and my nails done, what would be next? A dress? I stopped wearing dresses when I graduated from high school, and I hadn't worn all that many before. It was kind of a Joan of Arc thing—not that I hear voices or think of myself as a saint. But she believed that if you're going to ride with the soldiers, you have to dress like one. And then in the Inquisitors' prison, her male clothes provided both a kind of protection and a kind of strength. Dresses make you feel vulnerable. Classical women warriors always dressed the part.

I felt panicky at the thought of being forced into some kind of gender-determined role just because I wanted to see a man. Particularly when I didn't need a man, in any traditional sense. I owned my house and my business, and I got along just fine. So why, one night into something that may not go beyond two nights, was I already questioning my own center?

The Flamingo Hilton Beauty Salon was not reassuring. It was, as I had suspected, safely tucked away on the mezzanine—ground-floor space in Reno is too valuable to be used for anything but gambling devices. I had hoped for something small and friendly, and instead I got high-tech pink and white tile, too-bright fluorescent lights, and two rows of haircutting stations, one against each wall. Herds of people seemed to be milling about, wet-haired women in pink plastic ponchos, with streaked and permed teenagers in pink T-shirts and white pants nipping at their heels.

I almost turned and ran, but the permed, pink and white receptionist stopped me. She directed me to Barry, third station on the left. He was waiting, poised, hand on the back of a pink vinyl swivel chair in front of a very large mirror. He had declared his independence from the rest of the pink T-shirt crowd by not perming his streaked shoulder-length hair and by adding wide white suspenders to his ensemble. We exchanged hellos, I sat, and he started running his hands through my hair.

"What have you been shampooing with—lye?" he asked. "Your hair's so dry you're lucky it hasn't broken off at the roots. We can take care of that with a little conditioner—and you really must start using a moisturizer on your skin, darling, or you're going to age before your time. What else are we going to do with you?"

"I don't know—just trim it a little, shape it, I guess."

My skin did look dry in the harsh lights. And sallow. And blotchy. The freckles stood out. My eyebrows were too dark for my eyes, and I looked as if I didn't have any lashes. My chin turned from stubborn to pugnacious. I felt miserable and wanted to leave, but he had already whipped a pink cape around me and snapped it on.

"There's been some breakage that we'll have to snip off. For the rest, we could feather it a little, so it frames your face, and softens that chin."

He led me to a row of large basins in the back of the shop where he shampooed my hair, massaging my scalp and neck until I almost relaxed, and then left me lying there, dripping conditioner into the sink, for what felt like a day and a half. One of the smaller herders rinsed my hair, returned me to Barry, and brought me coffee.

As he trimmed my hair, one strand at a time, he kept up a running chatter, the way a dentist does when he has his hands in your mouth.

"You really have a marvelous natural look, darling, and

I adore your freckles. A little dab of transparent foundation, just to smooth out the colors a bit, would work wonders without spoiling the innocence of your face. And a tiny touch of mascara and lip gloss, that's really all you need. If you feel really daring, you might even try green mascara, to bring out that touch of green in your eyes. Your hair is almost a good color—I'll bet you were a towhead when you were a little girl, weren't you? Next time you come in we might add just a few blond highlights at the brow and temples. They'll pick up the natural color and blend right in. You're so lucky to have this much natural body, and you're going to be surprised at how much curl you have, once we give you a cut that follows the lines of your hair. You know, there's nothing wrong with having large hands, darling, particularly when you have such marvelously long fingers, but people can't help noticing them, and the cuticles could use a little attention. French manicures are *the* thing for the tailored look this season, and they'll give the illusion of length while your nails are growing out. At least you don't bite them, nothing looks worse than bitten nails, don't you think?''

The truly awful part was that at some point in his monologue I stopped feeling miserable and began to find him funny. By the time he was waving a blow dryer around my head with the panache of Luke Skywalker wielding a laser sword, I was even starting to like him.

''Shake your head, darling, and tell me what you think.''

Even though I had been following every step, I was stunned.

''It doesn't look like me.''

''It does look like you. There's a lioness inside you just dying to get out, and it's time you set her free. Give yourself some time to get used to it.''

''Are you sure I don't look like a shampoo ad with the wrong face under the hair?''

''Not at all. Now, when you do this at home, use your dryer to aerate the sides and back, a round brush to give a little height to the crown, and it'll fall right into place. Come see me again and let me know how it goes.''

''How what goes?''

''You do have a date this weekend, don't you? Isn't that why you got your hair done?''

I slunk out with my hands in my pockets, glancing furtively at my reflection in the mirrors that seem to be required decor for casinos. I did look a bit like a lioness, tall and rangy. I was going to have to decide if I wanted to.

Diane was the first person to see it, when I sat down at the Mother Lode counter.

''I like the hair, Freddie. Got something big going on?''

''No, not really,'' I said as casually as I could. ''Just thought it was time for a change.''

My first Keno ticket paid off seven of eight numbers—more money than Professor Hellman was paying me. The first time I had hit seven numbers in nine years, since the night I graduated from college. I got excited, thinking maybe it was an omen of some kind, but then I lost six games in succession. I was on my fourth beer, when Deke came in and sat down next to me.

''So. You want to tell me who he is?''

''Isn't the answer to that none of your business?'' I picked up my check, got up, and stopped for a moment. ''Have a good weekend, Deke, and I'll look for you Monday.''

There was, after all, some satisfaction in looking like a lioness.

Chapter
10

THE RED CORVETTE was in the driveway when I pulled up in front of Mick Halliday's house about midmorning on Friday. The house was in one of those upper-middle-class tracts, where the houses are all a little too big and a little too close together, and all painted the same shade of beige with the same sienna tile roofs and overwatered green lawns, and I always wonder why anyone with enough money to buy one of those homes would want to live in one.

The high-altitude sunrise had been so bright and rosy and clear, illuminating the vast open sky and desert, that for an instant I felt small, flying in a miniature airplane, with a Brobdingnagian world around me—reason enough to do it again sometime. I was so cheerful that I asked the rent-a-car agency for a Ford, and paid the extra two dollars a day to get it.

Mick didn't seem surprised to see me. He answered the door wearing gray velour sweats, with a cup of coffee in his hand. He didn't look as if he'd been up very long. His smile muscles weren't working yet.

"Changed your mind, have you, Freddie? I've still got your check."

"That's not it, Mick. I was hoping you might answer a few questions."

"Is somebody paying you to ask them?"

"Can I come in?"

"Of course you can. Come on in the kitchen, have a cup of coffee."

I followed him through a living room that looked as if it came intact from a model home, smooth furniture that no one ever sat in and silk flower displays, down the hall into a small, cheerful kitchen. He motioned me toward a breakfast nook. He took a brown stoneware mug from a cupboard and filled both it and his own with coffee from an automatic maker before he came over to join me.

"How can I help you?"

His smile muscles were starting to work a little better. But his eyes were too bloodshot for the message to reach them.

"You can tell me what happened. I sort of expected to be contacted for an inquest, and I wasn't. Everyone just zipped past all the formalities, and all of a sudden Joan was cremated and gone with no ceremony. I heard a rumor there might have been some pressure from somewhere, and I figured if there was, you could tell me about it."

"No pressure—and no disagreement, either. The police had your statement, and they didn't see any reason to call you back. They saw the case as open and shut. I think they talked to her therapist, that was all they needed. And maybe I was wrong, but I wanted to get through this as quickly as possible, with as little fanfare as possible, and I couldn't face the charade of a ceremony. I'm not a religious person, so I didn't see the need for one."

"Would you give me the name of her therapist?"

"Michael Houston. He's in some medical building in North Las Vegas, I guess I could look up the address for you."

"That's okay. I can look it up myself." I paused to take a sip of my coffee. "You know, Mick, I could maybe buy the story that Joan killed Lois and then took too many pills when she was upset, except for one thing."

"What's that?"

"Charlie thinks somebody was trying to kill him, and

he's scared of something. Why would he be scared, if there's nobody after him?''

Mick's laugh sounded genuine.

"Charlie? You're worried about Charlie? He's an old man, and he's scared of dying, so he sees monsters in the shadows, that's all. He's going to die anyway—why would someone be in a hurry?''

"I don't know. But I thought you might—I thought that might have been why you tried to buy me off twice.''

"I never tried to buy you off, Freddie. I've always been fond of you, since you were eight years old and scared of the water, and I just wanted you to have a little something out of all this. I'm not very good with money—it withers like rose petals in my hands—and I may have been a little clumsy in offering you some. I'll tell you what—take back the check and then do what you like. Explore, don't explore, ask questions, go home. Do what makes you comfortable. How's that?''

"I don't know, Mick. I'm not sure.''

"Sure you're sure. Don't worry about it. I'll win it back tonight. Did I tell you I'm a professional poker player these days?''

"No, you didn't. Sounds like a tough way to make a living.''

"Unpredictable. But then so's being a private eye.''

"True.'' I was starting to believe him. I wanted to believe him. I just had to ask one more thing. "By the way, do you know anything about Castle Properties—or how Charlie might be connected to Castle Properties?''

"I don't recall that I've ever heard of the firm. Why?''

Nothing wavered, not the smile, not the eyelids, not the hand that held the coffee mug.

"Just wondered. Just wondered.''

"Hang on a minute,'' he said, and bounced up from his chair and out into the hall in one movement.

I looked out the window at a small patch of grass so green I was certain nobody had let it know it didn't belong in the desert. The grass ended abruptly at a cement-block fence. In

contrast, three African violets on the windowsill were
sagging, as if no one had remembered to water them in a
while. I took them over to the sink and drenched them,
because I felt I had to do something. Mick returned as I was
shutting off the water.

"What a nice thing to do—they were Joan's, of course,
and I'm afraid I didn't notice they were getting dry. Here."
He tucked the check into the pocket of my jacket. "Now
that's settled. Sit down and have another cup of coffee."

"Mick, I have a client, and taking a check from you may
be a conflict of interest."

"Okay. How's this? Take it. But don't cash it until you're
satisfied that I'm innocent of whatever it is you suspect
me of. If you find I've done something re-pre-hen-sible"—
he mocked me with the word—"tear it up."

"That's a deal. And thanks."

"You're welcome. Time for another cup?"

"No. Thank you. I have a couple more stops to make."

"And plans for later, I can tell you have plans for later."

"What do you mean?"

"There's color in your cheeks, and you've had your hair
cut. You look lovely, Freddie, and I envy the man."

That was enough to put color in my cheeks—all the way
from my collarbone to my forehead. I left as gracefully as I
could, the check burning a hole in my pocket. I knew taking
it wasn't a good idea. But I wouldn't cash it as long as I was
working on the case, and then I could see how I felt about
it. Truth be known, I could use the money.

I found a public telephone at a gas station a few blocks
away and looked up Michael Houston in the directory.

"Mr. Houston has left for the weekend," a warm female
voice informed me. "Is this an emergency?"

"No, but I need to talk with him as soon as I can. I'm a
private investigator, and I need to ask him some questions.
Will he be in the office Monday?"

"Yes, but I'm not sure he'll be willing to talk with you,
not if you want information about a client."

"The situation is a little tricky," I admitted. "When do you think I could call and catch him?"

"Is there someplace he could call you?"

"I don't think so."

There was a pause while she thought about my request.

"He won't be in before afternoon, when he sees his first client, and then he's booked straight through until eight. You might try to catch him about five till eight."

"Thanks."

I took Cheyenne to Decatur Boulevard and swung around to Bonanza Road. I dreaded the thought of bearding Aunt Mae in her den, but I felt I had to try one more time. As I turned onto Aunt Mae's block, I saw a woman with a bag of groceries step onto the porch. By the time I parked in front, she was inside and the door was closed. I wasn't sure I was glad to know somebody was home.

I knocked, waited, knocked again. One more time, Aunt Mae opened the door until the chain caught.

"What you want?"

"I'm still looking for Mary Yates, and I wondered if you had ever given her my card, let her know that she might have some money coming."

"I don't know no Mary Yates."

Somebody mumbled something inside the house. Aunt Mae pulled back, shutting the door, but not tight. When the door reopened, Mary Yates was there.

"What is this?" Her voice was low and quiet. "Nobody be leaving me any money, except maybe Mr. Barrington, and last I heard he wasn't dead. So why are you looking for me and what do you want?"

"I'm looking into the murders of Mr. Barrington's two daughters, and I don't suspect you of anything, but I was hoping you could help me answer some questions."

"Murders" threw her. Whatever she was expecting, it wasn't that. She was hesitating, and I thought maybe she was going to give me some kind of answer, when suddenly she looked at something over my shoulder. Before I could turn, the something had me in a partial bear hug with his left arm, and his right hand had a knife at my throat.

"Don't move, girl, or you'll get blood on your shirt," the something hissed in my ear. The blast of stale whiskey breath almost triggered my gag reflex.

I didn't exactly move. I'm real careful when somebody with a knife edge pressing my skin gives me that kind of instruction. I sagged against him, just enough so that I could shift closer to the left. My right hand ended up precisely between his thighs, and a quick grab found his balls. I squeezed, pulled, and twisted in one motion. He made a funny sound, sort of an "uhnnnh," as he dropped the knife and went down to his knees. My elbow caught him in the neck, just enough to choke him up on his way down. I turned and saw a black man with glasses and a goatee, who was turning indigo before my eyes.

Mary Yates slammed the door. I picked up the knife and sprinted for the car before she could call for reinforcements. No way would she answer questions after that.

I was at the junction of Main and Las Vegas Boulevard before I allowed myself to start shaking. One of the few advantages to being a woman in this business is that most of the tough guys you run into are so dumb it doesn't occur to them that you've studied self-defense. You don't even need to be very good at it. And I'm not. Or if I am, it's only as good as I have to be, so that I don't get hurt. I don't have a uniform with a belt, or anything like that. That's turning it into a game, too much like making it fun. Hurting someone should never be fun.

I was early, and I didn't want to meet Lucas while I was still shaking, so I turned back to 15 and headed north, taking the long way, through the Valley of Fire. Driving isn't nearly as good as flying for burning the carbon out of your soul, but it's the second best thing.

I stopped and bought a can of beer from a young Indian woman at the Moapa Tribal Outpost and pulled off at Atlatl Rock to drink it, to sit and shiver until I was calm and feeling more or less okay. The massive rocks were the raw color of fresh blood, as if Zeus had launched his thunderbolts at the earth, and the gashes had erupted and hardened, not scar tissue, but proud flesh turned to stone.

The afternoon was over by the time I turned toward Echo Bay, and Lucas was locking the door to the shop when he saw me get out of the car.

"Howya doin'?" he asked, smiling. "Good to see you."

I blushed when I saw him, remembering his body. He glanced away and put the keys in his pocket.

"I don't know how I'm doing. I don't know what I'm doing. Every time I think I know what game I'm playing, what the rules are, something shifts."

"You need to find out what game the other guys are playing."

"Yeah, that's what I've been trying to do, and I almost got myself hurt doing it."

"Want to tell me?"

We were walking down to Dock D as we talked. That first moment had been awkward, seeing him, I had expected that. But then it wasn't awkward anymore. I just started telling him what had happened, and it was okay. He didn't say anything except "Want a beer?" until we were sitting in a couple of deck chairs watching the sunset.

"Okay," he said, swallowing about a quarter of a can, "it bothers me."

"What?"

"That you had to take out a guy with a knife this afternoon. I'm proud of you, that you could do it, but it bothers me that you had to."

"Are you really? Proud?"

"Yeah, sure I am. I like it that you're good at what you do. I also like it that you're surprised to discover that. But I like *you,* and I don't want you to step over the wrong line and get hurt, and it bothers me that you might."

I didn't know what to say, so I just looked at him. He was wearing a plaid shirt and jeans again. Given the limited space in a houseboat, he probably didn't have too many choices. His feet, in worn sneakers, were propped up on the rail. The beer can dangled from a large hand at the end of a beefy forearm. I had found out, last time, that he was solid, not soft. He was one of those men who wouldn't look right if he lost weight, he needed the heft to balance broad shoulders and a barrel chest.

"Who are you?" I finally asked.

"Lucas Hecht," he answered, smiling at me.

"No, come on. All we've done is talk about me, or the case that I'm wrapped up in right now, and I just realized I don't know who you are or how you came here. Or why you named your boat Second Chance."

"Good name for a boat, isn't it."

"Yes."

I waited.

"Oh, hell, I don't know what to say. I'm just a guy who likes to fish and found a way to do it."

"Who did you used to be?"

"My previous incarnation, as the New Agers would put it, was as a stockbroker."

"What did you do—make a lot of money and retire early?"

"I made a lot of money. I spent a lot, too. I thought that was what life was about—make it and spend it. I had a wife who thought that was what life was about, too."

"What was she like?"

"Smart. Pretty. Ambitious. When I met her, she was a nineteen-year-old bank teller, working her way through college. I was in the midst of a white-knuckled ride through the roller-coaster stock market of the seventies. She thought it was fun. We got married when she graduated, and for the next three years she had a long commute to USC law school. After that, the good times rolled."

"So what stopped them?"

I was getting a little tense, hearing about his smart, pretty, ambitious wife.

"I'm still not sure, and I've given it a lot of thought. The easy label is the October '87 crash. We had forgotten—all of us living off the bull market—what a crash was like, fooled ourselves into thinking it wouldn't happen again. And all we had to do was reread Benjamin Graham."

"Who was Benjamin Graham?"

"One of the old market gurus, a generation or so ago. He said, 'They always tell you it's going to be different this time. It never is.' But it feels different, of course, every time. Every uptrend is going to last forever, and every downtick is a disaster. But the eighties were straight up, and greed was in, and I really did forget that the bull market couldn't last forever. And then all I could think of, that Tuesday morning after the five-hundred-point drop in the Dow, was that I couldn't face a return to the bad old days of the late seventies, the days of phone calls to tell people you liked, people who trusted you, that they were worth half today of what they were worth last month. They could do that to themselves on the roulette table, and I wouldn't have to watch."

He drained the can, got up, and returned with two more.

"You cared too much."

"Yeah, that's what my wife said. She said you have to be able to face a little blood without fainting, as long as it's someone else's. And I just didn't want to do it."

"So?"

"So I told her I needed to get away for a little while, think about what I was going to do, and I came out here and rented a houseboat, and then I bought a houseboat, and then six months had passed, and the guy with the bait and tackle shop wanted to retire. I told her I was buying the shop. She said good-bye."

"Are you sorry—now that you know the October crash wasn't the beginning of the end of the world?"

"Hell, no. I wouldn't go back if they paid me—and actually, they would."

"But is this what you want to do every day for the rest of your life—fish?"

That's wasn't a good thing to ask. Things all of a sudden got awkward.

"I don't know what I want to do for the rest of my life. This is what I want to do now—fish. If I wake up one morning and I don't want to go fishing, I'll think about doing something else."

"You didn't like that question. I'm sorry."

"It's okay."

A moment of silence was enough for the tension to ease. Desert sunsets are soft, gentle, pastel colors, mostly shades of pink. Riotous city sunsets are caused by reflections of light off the various pollutants in the air. This was the first pink sunset I'd watched in a while, and it was making me feel soft and gentle, too.

"Any more questions?" he asked.

"What's for dinner?"

"I don't know. Let's go see."

He held out his hand and I took it. Gladly.

As we started inside, he stopped and kissed me.

"I like your hair," he said, running his hand over my cheek and ear and into my hair. "I noticed when I saw you, and I would have said something then, but I wanted to know what was bothering you, and then I forgot."

I went stiff.

"What?" he asked.

"I don't know. I'm not sure how much I'm willing to change for you, that's all."

"Change?" He went stiff. "Who asked you to change? Whatever happens between us is not going to be about somebody changing, me or you. I liked you when I met you, just the way you were. And all I said tonight was that I liked your hair, and if you didn't want me to comment, you should have warned me."

"You're right. I'm sorry."

He dropped my hand.

"I'll put the coals on."

Nothing like a little tension to spoil a romantic mood.

He piled the coals into a neat pyramid around an electric starter, then opened two more beers and handed me one.

"Can I ask another question?"

"If you're feeling brave."

I wasn't, but I went ahead anyway.

"Is there some way to get information about a private corporation that I haven't thought of?"

"Nope. There is no way to get information about a private corporation unless you can get somebody on the inside to talk. Or you break into their files." He paused and looked at me. "Shit. I didn't say that. You don't break into their files, ever."

"Of course I don't. Besides, I haven't given up trying to get somebody on the inside to talk. It's just that I'm not sure who's on the inside and who isn't."

"What about Charlie? Where do you think he is?"

"I don't know. If Castle Properties is behind this—and I don't even know that they are—then he either is on the inside, was on the inside, or knows who's on the inside. But it doesn't matter which because he won't talk to me."

"Maybe if you're lucky they'll make a direct attempt on his life."

"You don't think Lois was a mistake? You think they were really after her?"

"Well—you're my filter on this, of course, because I wasn't there, but I like Julie's theory, that this is slow torture. If it is, they'll do something else."

"What?"

"How would I know? Whose death would make things worse—as in more frightening for Charlie?"

"God, I don't know. He doesn't seem to care about anybody. Not even his daughters, he didn't even care much about them."

"That must have been tough for them. But fathers don't sometimes, care much about daughters, particularly his generation. What was your relationship with your father? Who was he?''

''Lucas, I don't want to talk about my father. Okay?''

''Okay.''

He unplugged the starter, pulled it from the coals, and dipped the end in the water. It sizzled as it cooled. Then he rebuilt the neat pyramid, this time using tongs.

''You know,'' he said, ''unless we can find a safe topic of conversation, we may end up spending the entire night on the deck.''

''Maybe we shouldn't talk for a while.''

This time I held out my hand. He took it.

Dinner was grilled corn, zucchini, and onions, and a big channel catfish that he fileted carefully. He made his own tartar sauce, too. I couldn't imagine making my own tartar sauce, simple as it looked. We stayed on the really safe background stuff—where did you go to school, what books did you like—all through dinner.

''So,'' he said, after he had washed the plates and utensils—grilling doesn't use too many things—and we were both back in our deck chairs, another beer in hand. ''Do you want to stick around down here until Monday— when you see the shrink?''

''I hadn't thought about it, one way or the other.'' That was a lie. ''That's a lie, I've thought about it, I just wasn't sure what you would want. Or what I would want.''

''I'd like it if you stayed.''

''Okay. I'll stay.''

''What about your cats?''

''I left enough dry food and water for the weekend, because I wasn't sure how long I'd be gone. And they are, unfortunately, great hunters. Both of them. They'll be fine until Monday. I'll fly back Monday night.''

''That doesn't worry you—flying a small plane at night?''

''Sometimes when it's dark, but not when there's a full moon.''

''Okay. Good. Want to turn in early?''

I couldn't remember the last time I had spent three full days that qualified as vacation. I was due.

Everybody has a fantasy about what a romantic weekend ought to be like. And like the commercial for Club Med vacations, they're all different. This one fit mine: time together, talking, touching, eating, and sleeping—fortunately Lucas could cook more than fish—and time alone, because he didn't want to close the shop for the entire weekend. I took a couple of long walks along the edge of the lake, but mostly I just sat in a deck chair, watching silver-sprayed water-skiers shimmer past, hoping I would never have to move quickly again.

I didn't forget entirely about the case. I walked up to the ranger station to see if Tom could add anything to what I already knew. He couldn't. He'd been dropped from the loop, just as I had been. Except that he was glad—nobody at Echo Bay wanted the kind of attention a dead body usually brings.

The Queen of Hearts was still in her slip, her bright paint a jaunty veneer over the already-present aura of abandonment. I wondered how long it would be before the rumors started that the houseboat was haunted. And whether Mick would sell it first.

Lucas confirmed that Mick had moved everything out and had put the houseboat up for sale. None of the locals wanted it.

I was hoping something—anything—would be clearer at the end of the weekend than it was at the beginning, but no such luck. No answers had sprung forth magically from my relaxed psyche, about either my relationship with Lucas Hecht or a solution to the case. I knew flying down that I liked Lucas and was nervous about a relationship. Now I had the added information that Lucas liked me and was nervous about a relationship, although somewhat less nervous than I was. About the case, I didn't even have more information.

The beginning of the weekend hadn't been awkward, but

the end made up for it. We just stood there and stared at each other, all the intimacy of passion somehow dissipated in the white afternoon light. I picked up my flight bag and tossed it over my shoulder.

"Well," I started lamely. "Thanks for the weekend. It was really great."

"Yeah, sure. Thank you for coming. Let me carry that to the car for you."

"What? No, no, I can do it. Thanks anyway."

"I'll walk out with you."

"Okay."

We trudged to the parking lot in silence.

"I don't know when—or whether—I'll have to fly back down. But I'll call you when I know. Do you ever come to Reno?"

"Not often. But I'll call you."

The drive back to Las Vegas along the misnamed North Shore Road was long and empty. I felt as if I had left something important behind. I didn't know quite what it was, but I knew I couldn't go back for it.

I found the building where Michael Houston's office lurked about seven-thirty. It was a fairly modern, medium high-rise building with a pharmacy and a coffee shop on the ground floor. I grabbed a cup of coffee and went upstairs to wait. I was cheered to note that the initials after his name were MA, MFCC. I know that every licensed therapist swears that what takes place with a client is confidential, most of them stick to it, and Marriage, Family and Child Counselor is a legitimate and useful license. I also know that psychiatrists are the stickiest of the bunch, and that as the education goes down, the accessibility goes up.

A sad, halting elevator took me to the fourth floor. Houston shared a suite of offices with three other persons, all with several initials after their names indicating degrees and licenses of one kind or another. The anteroom was cramped, barely enough room for a table and two aging overstuffed chairs, upholstered in something that was brown in the worn spots and plum around the edges. The table held a lamp—the only illumination—and a handful of old magazines.

Next to the inside door was a grid of names and buttons. I pressed the one next to Michael Houston, then sat down to wait. He opened the door about nine minutes to eight. I was further cheered to note that he looked young, eager, and kind.

"You must be Miss O'Neal," he said, extending his hand. I rose from the chair and extended my own. He came maybe to my shoulder, but looking up at me didn't seem to bother him. "My secretary told me that you might call. I see you decided to stop by instead."

"I didn't want to do this over the phone. I thought it might be easier to talk in person."

"Of course. Follow me."

The inner offices seemed to have been divided into the smallest possible spaces. The door he opened for me led into a room with a chair, a couch, and a table. A box of Kleenex sat on the table. I considered taking the chair, just to see if it would throw him, but I sat down on the couch, firmly, feet on the floor.

"I wanted to ask you some questions about Joan Halliday."

He frowned and looked away.

"Hey, I've never lost a client before either," I told him.

"That's very perceptive of you, Miss O'Neal. And also an attempt to establish a bond between us, I would think." The frown softened, to something rueful. "Now, what is your interest in Joan Halliday?"

I told him she had hired me for help after her sister's death, and then another relative had hired me when she died. Period.

"Yes. It was after her sister's unfortunate death that I first saw her."

"Do you mind if I ask—why did she come to you?"

"You mean rather than someone with more reputation? I was recommended by a former client, Lucas Hecht."

My vital organs quit working. No air flowed through my lungs, no blood through my heart. My voice whispered out.

"Lucas Hecht?"

"Yes. He and his wife were clients of mine. That's upset you, and I'm sorry. In fact, I probably shouldn't have mentioned his name, but he's always been so open about having seen me, and seemed pleased with the working relationship, even though he and Barbara did ultimately divorce, and—I'm sorry. Do you want to tell me about it?"

"No, no, I don't think so." I tried to laugh, but it was a strange, nervous sound. "I just want to know about Joan Halliday."

He sighed. His hands fluttered.

"This is such a problem, patient-therapist confidentiality is a serious issue, you must know that."

"I do. And murder is a serious issue. Both Joan and her sister Lois have been murdered, I believe that, and I think someone is trying to close the case as a murder-suicide. If you have information that can help me keep it open, it would mean a lot to me. And it might help Joan Halliday's ghost rest."

"Yes. If you believe in ghosts, of course."

I waited.

"What do you want to know?" he asked, just when I was about to give up and break the silence.

"She didn't kill her sister, did she?"

"She said she didn't, and I believe her."

"Was she depressed at all—suicidal?"

"No, she wasn't."

I winced, and he noticed, but we both let it go.

"What kind of a problem did she want professional help with?"

"A—conflict. She had information, and she didn't know what to do with it, and she was afraid, afraid to talk and afraid not to."

"Did she tell you the precise nature of this information?"

"No."

"Did she tell you who she was afraid of?"

"No."

"Damn."

Both of us managed to smile, but weakly.

"But I think it involved her father," he added.

"Well, thanks, I guess. Anything else?"

"Not really. She didn't see me very long—only a few times—and then she didn't show up for her appointment, and when I called to find out what happened, her husband told me she was dead, accidental overdose."

"Did the police contact you?"

"No—no, they didn't talk to me."

"Okay. I guess that's it."

I tried to get up, but I felt glued to the couch, weighted to the floor.

"Miss O'Neal—please—I know I upset you, and I didn't mean to. The first rule of the healing professions is 'Do no harm.' Are you sure you don't want to talk with me about it?"

"No. Thank you. I need to think about it. But thank you for offering."

I left as gracefully as I could, which was not very. I thought about driving back to Echo Bay and confronting Lucas, but I was tired and hurting and couldn't face it. I sat in the coffee shop for an hour, and I finally picked up a pay phone.

"You lied," I said when he answered. "You lied to me."

There was silence.

"I didn't lie," he said after a pause so long I thought he might have walked away. "Not exactly. I just didn't tell you everything. I withheld, as a psychologist might put it."

"No, you didn't. You lied. You said you barely knew her, that all you talked about was the weather."

"Yeah, well, I guess we talked more than that."

"Why did you lie? Were you her lover or something?"

''Not or something, just her lover.''

I hung up. I couldn't manage good-bye.

I saw a sign pointing back toward Henderson before I realized I'd missed the turnoff to the airport.

By the time I took off, it was almost ten o'clock. The sensible thing to do would have been to stay the night in Las Vegas, but I wasn't feeling sensible. I was feeling a need to be back in my own bed, with Butch and Sundance curled up tight against me. There was some light cloud cover, so I headed up to 10,500 feet, higher than I normally would have flown, but I wanted to take advantage of the full moon.

About half an hour out of Las Vegas, I began to calm down. When Lucas hadn't told me at the beginning that he was Joan Halliday's lover, there was no good time to do it. I could see that, sort of. But it didn't stop me from feeling hurt and betrayed. Or wondering what else he had ''withheld.''

And what about Mick? If someone—Joan or Lucas or a nosy neighbor—had failed to withhold the information from Mick, he had a very personal motive for murder. But it didn't matter. Even if I could tie him to Joan's death—which I couldn't—I still couldn't tie him to Lois's death, or to Charlie's fear.

The mountain ridge out the window meandering away to my left poked through the clouds like a ghostly salamander. The moon was a fat round searchlight, lighting up the world so no one could sneak up on me. They felt like company, as if I weren't traveling alone. Now, over the desert, away from the cloud cover, I could see—what I could see was Highway 95 to my left, where it shouldn't have been. And that mountain salamander had wandered too far off. I had been so upset about Lucas that I forgot to reset the heading system. I cross-checked it against the Whiskey compass. I was flying about twenty degrees too far east.

I started to correct my course. But that was the moment I heard the first sputter.

I thought it was a mistake—that my ears had sputtered,

not the engine. By the second sputter, I knew it wasn't a mistake. I checked the gauges, the oil pressure. The tanks showed almost full, and I couldn't find any indication of anything wrong. But the sputter became a death rattle. The engine quit.

I fought the panic. This wasn't serious, it couldn't be.

I reached down to trim, put the nose down, and set up for a ninety-knot glide. Then I tried an air start. Nothing happened when I turned the key. I fought the panic again. I was going to have to glide to a landing, somewhere close.

I pulled out the charts and found where I thought I might be on the sectional, looking for a possible spot. If I was close enough to Tonopah—that light ahead might be, had to be Tonopah, nothing else in the middle of Nevada was that big—I might be able to deadstick it into Mud Lake. If Mud Lake was dry. I set the glide, switched the squawk to 7700, and turned on the radio.

"Tonopah, Tonopah, can you read me?"

This was late for Tonopah. The Flight Service Center usually closed early. My voice quavered. I worked to steady it.

"Tonopah, Tonopah, this is November eight-one-nine-four Whiskey, do you read me?"

Static, nothing but damn static.

Impending death strips away thoughts of anything but itself. I was empty of everything but two choices: I could fall peacefully into the last cold embrace, or I could figure out how the story would have to be written if I was going to live, and then make it happen that way. For a moment I was tempted to fall. Giving up was easier, and it would be quick. I could head for the mountain ridge, go up in flames, gloriously. The last burning embrace. There were worse ways to die. I was sure of that, even though at the moment I couldn't think of any.

Living meant I had to find Mud Lake—which ought to be right off my nose. I was coming through 8,000 feet, I had about three miles of glide, and I wasn't sure if I was imagining the glimmer ahead. And if I couldn't get an answer from Tonopah, I would just have to land somehow and use the beacon in the Cherokee's tail to get help. I could survive this. I had to survive this.

"Tonopah, Tonopah, this is November eight-one-nine-four Whiskey, declaring in-flight emergency, can you read?"

Tears started down my face, but my voice had steadied, and my hands held the yoke.

"November eight-one-nine-four Whiskey, this is Tonopah, give us your location."

I heard the scratchy voice, and almost blasted the radio with my response.

"Tonopah, dear God, Tonopah, I'm about thirty miles south-southeast, seven thousand feet up, engine out. I'm going to try for Mud Lake."

"Ninety-four Whiskey, we'll scramble a helicopter from Test Range. Have you ever made an emergency landing before?"

"That's a joke, right, Tonopah?"

"Ninety-four Whiskey, an emergency landing is no joke. Have you tried an air start?"

"Yes, sir. And the flaps are down. Anything else, Tonopah?"

"Ninety-four Whiskey, watch your speed, remember you have plenty of time. Keep your nose down, Whiskey, below the horizon. Don't bleed off your speed. Gain your best glide."

The glimmer off the nose became a blast of white.

"Tonopah—I see it—it looks dry, no water."

"Ninety-four Whiskey, confirming the lake is dry."

"The wind—what's the wind, Tonopah?"

"Ninety-four Whiskey, wind is calm. Watch your speed, Whiskey, don't get too slow, and keep your nose down."

"I'm there, Tonopah, I'm right at the edge of the lake, about eight hundred feet up."

"Ninety-four Whiskey, look for the spot where you want to land. Remember your depth perception is off at night, and keep your eye on the spot you've picked. Now you can pull the nose up, slowly, bleed off your air speed, but don't flare too soon.''

Static.

''Tonopah—are you still there?''

''Ninety-four Whiskey, I'm here, take it easy, baby, you have time, and I'll wait up for you.''

I trimmed, nose up, nose up, I was pulling back, pulling back, harder and harder on the yoke, now slippery from the sweat on my palms, as the alkali bed came closer and closer.

Gliding down so silently, so smoothly, I had only known from the dials how rapidly I was falling, praying that the wings on either side, holding me fast, were those of an eagle, not those of the Angel of Death.

A bump, a shudder, and another bump. The shriek as the plane's landing gear touched alkali ripped apart the silence, and I couldn't even hear my own scream until the sliding, skewing sound stopped.

''Ninety-four Whiskey? Are you there? Come on, baby, answer me! Ninety-four Whiskey, come in!''

''Tonopah, this is Ninety-four Whiskey.''

''Jesus, Ninety-four Whiskey, talk to me. Are you all right?''

''I don't know. Give me a minute to check.''

I disengaged my hands from the yoke, one finger at a time. Then I started touching myself, touching my face, my breast, my arms, my body, needing to know that I was still flesh, still solid. I checked muscles after that, muscles in my back, in my legs. I twitched my toes.

''Tonopah? I think I'm okay.''

Just at the periphery of my hearing was a faint hum. At first I thought it was madness.

''Tonopah? Is that the helicopter?''

''Ninety-four Whiskey, you are one lucky broad. The drinks are on me.''

Chapter
11

"BROKEN FUEL HOSE," the pilot of the rescue helicopter said, peering under the cowling with the aid of his flashlight. "Looks like the clamp is missing. Nothing serious. You can replace it in the morning and be on your way."

He dropped me at the Flight Service Center, where Tonopah had indeed waited up for me. Tonopah turned out to be a retired Air Force colonel who hung out at the airport, real name Paul, warm and friendly and talkative, tall, still lean, with a horsy face and an iron-gray brushcut.

By the second beer at the Hotel Mizpah bar I was getting over the shock of the landing. Every muscle in my body was sore—especially the ones in my arms, the ones that had kept pulling back on the yoke—but I was feeling glad to be alive, even in a Tonopah bar. Paul was feeling proud of both of us, and I could see the story taking shape the third time he told it to the bartender. He was already planning the movie, starring Sean Connery and Sigourney Weaver. I told him he could have the rights.

Paul insisted on picking me up the next morning, new fuel hose in hand, and driving me out to the plane. As I checked out of the motel—the Mizpah reminded me too much of something in a horror novel, I never could have slept there—I remembered that this was Tuesday, and I was supposed to be lunching with Sandra Herrick in Reno. I called both the *Herald* and Harrah's coffee shop, hoping that one of the messages would get to her. As a backup, I left a message on her home machine.

"Perfect landing, Whiskey, we did a great job," Paul chortled as we bounced onto the alkali flat in his ATV.

He was a little less sanguine after we examined the fuel hose. The end had been cut with a knife. Somebody had loosened the clamp and split the end of the fuel hose, so that the engine vibration would shake it free at some point during my trip. The gas would still be in the tanks, but it wouldn't reach the carburetor. No gas, no engine. And almost no pilot.

"Somebody wanted you dead, Whiskey."

I had known that. I had known it, and I hadn't wanted to face it, not even when the helicopter pilot had told me the clamp was missing. The fear I had felt in the silent plane flooded my heart all over again. I waited for the pounding to stop before I answered.

"Well, we sure fooled them, didn't we, Tonopah?"

He frowned.

"Is there something I can do? I'm going to have to tell the FAA, you know that."

"I know—and that's okay, I'd love to have the FAA involved, anybody involved. I'm not doing anything illegal, that's not what this is about. I just think somebody else may be. And I don't think you can do any more to help than you've already done. And God—" I had to stop again for a moment. "I'm grateful, really. If I think of something else you can do, I'll call you."

"How about coming back for another beer once you've solved the case—I think I deserve to know the rest of the story."

"You got it."

I'd never taken off from an alkali flat before, but it was a lot easier than the landing. I was nervous at first, shaky, in fact, and I kept listening to the engine, more than I normally would, but by the time I asked Reno Ground Clearance for permission to land, it was business as usual. Except for one thing. I'd never seen beauty in the airport before, but that afternoon the backlight from the sun was just right, and it glowed as though someone were shooting it through a soft filter lens. The lights of the runway twinkled like evening stars.

I had asked Paul to let Jerry McIntire know what happened—I knew I was going to have to talk to him, but I wasn't sure how many times I could face telling the story in the first twenty-four hours, and he wasn't high on my priority list—so I slipped into the parking lot, picked up my car, and split for home.

Butch was sitting on the front porch as I parked. He waited, glaring, until I was almost upon him, and then took off around the corner of the house. As I opened the front door, I was greeted by the stink of dead quail. What appeared from the topknots and feet to be the remains of three bodies littered my office carpet.

Sundance was startled out of his late afternoon nap when I dropped my flight bag on the bed. He yawned, stretched, and eased over to be petted, apparently unaware that I had been gone for four days. Certainly unaware that I almost hadn't made it back. I picked him up and hugged him, needing the security of his purr against my chest. I sat for a moment, to think what to do next, and he was instantly asleep again.

The phone rang, but it was too far away, so I let the machine answer it.

"Freddie, it's Rob." The familiar voice floated down the hall. "I just heard from Jerry that you had to make an emergency landing in the desert. I hope you're okay. Call me sometime."

I absolutely could not handle that call. And I didn't think I'd call him sometime.

Checking messages. That was what I needed to do, as soon as I had the strength to move Sundance off my lap, walk down the hall to my office, and hit the playback button.

A message from Professor Hellman wanting to know how things were going, one to call my insurance company, one from Sandra Herrick hoping I was all right, and one from Lucas Hecht, who wanted to talk.

I called Sandra.

"What are you doing in Tonopah with plane trouble?" she asked.

"Not now, it's too complicated. Can we reschedule lunch for tomorrow?"

"Sure. How was your weekend in Vegas—or was that complicated, too?"

"As a matter of fact, it was. I'll tell you when I see you—noon tomorrow at Harrah's."

I opened a beer and cleaned up the quail remains.

Sanity lies in order and routine. I decided to walk to the Mother Lode for a hamburger.

Diane plopped a beer in front of me.

"So how was your date?"

"Okay, I guess. Have you seen Deke?"

"Not since Friday. Thought maybe you two ran off together."

"Not likely."

"I see you're back to the ponytail. I really did like your hair loose—you ought to get it done more often."

"Yeah, thanks, I'll think about it. How about a hamburger?"

"Sure thing."

I was halfway through the hamburger and my third Keno ticket when Deke sat down beside me.

"You want to talk?" he asked.

"Well, one of us ought to."

"Both of us. You first."

"Somebody fucked with my plane."

I told him about the slit fuel hose, listened to his speech about how I ought to quit all this and get married and have babies, and then I told him about Mick and Mary Yates and the shrink. I skipped the attack, because I wasn't up for another speech. I thought about mentioning Lucas, but that still didn't seem any of Deke's business.

"What about you?" I ended. "How was your weekend?"

"Not nearly so exciting as yours. Feeding the ducks can't compare to no plane crash."

"It wasn't a crash. Just an emergency landing."

"Suppose you'd been on course, between airports, without no Air Force colonel on the radio?"

"There were other places besides Mud Lake to land—I admit a little smaller and a little harder to find at night, but they're there. And the Air Force colonel didn't tell me much I didn't already know. I could have made it anyway. It just would have been a long walk home."

"And you might not have made it anyway. One broken leg and you can't walk very far."

"Stop that. You sound as if you're sorry it wasn't worse."

"I'm not. I just want you to know how serious it was. Somebody messing around with you, who means it."

"You can let up, and I can order another beer, or I can leave."

"Diane, get this woman another beer, and put it on my check," he called.

Diane brought the beer, smiling, but left quickly when she realized we were glaring at each other.

"Okay," he said, when I had taken a sip, and he knew I was staying. "Stephanie is a sweet child, and she is going to be okay, but she says her mother is involved with one bad dude."

"That's Willie Carver?"

"Right."

"Is that all you found out? That Willie Carver is a bad dude? As if we didn't know that already?"

"Stephanie don't know too much about her mama's

business. She know a little, though—like they never have to look for a place to live. Her mama call some number, and then they have a place to go. Sometimes they have to move in a hurry, but they always have another place.''

"She doesn't know the number."

"No."

"And one of the places they moved was in with Charlie Barrington."

"Looks that way."

"Does Stephanie know anything about anybody dealing drugs?''

"No, but she say it wouldn't surprise her."

"Anything more?"

"That's it."

"Yeah, well, thanks. Thanks for the beer, too."

Lunch the next day with Sandra Herrick was only a little more successful.

This time she was wearing a full, flowery, crinkle-cotton skirt with a turquoise sweater, same heavy gold jewelry.

"Well, it's curious," she said as she sat down.

"What?"

"There's no reference to Castle Properties on the Woodruff Wallace computers, and none in Hank d'Arbanville's papers. At least, not *our* Hank d'Arbanville. But Don found one reference to an investment in Castle Properties among Hank *Senior*'s papers."

"That's the father?"

"Right. And when Don told Van Woodruff's secretary he was looking for the Castle Properties file, she told him that he'd have to ask Van for it—that he kept it in a locked drawer."

"I don't suppose he did—ask Van for it."

"Not likely."

"Tell me about Hank Senior. I know he opened the Paiute Inn, but that's about it."

"Just a small-town Basque innkeeper—except that the

town was Carson City, and the hotel-casino does well enough to finance Hank Junior's forays into politics.''

"Does he still live in Carson? Can you get me an address?''

"I think so, and I'll see. So what have you got for me?''

I gave her the same information I had given Deke.

"Are you scared?'' she asked. "You must be scared, I know I would be.''

I was more afraid of saying I was scared than anything else. I was afraid if I said it, it would get too real.

"I suppose I would be if I thought about it. But that might stop me, and I can't let that happen.''

"They may try something else.''

"And they may not—if I'm right and Castle Properties is behind this—if too many people know about it. They won't want the investigation. They'll figure they can stop me another way. Besides, if part of this is to scare Charlie, they've already done that.''

"But he doesn't know.''

"He will after lunch—he's my next stop.''

We settled down to salads and coffee and easier conversation. Except it almost wasn't easier—I kept stifling an impulse to confide in her, tell her about Lucas, and I wasn't sure why I wanted to do that.

Finally I blurted, "Look—do you want to hear about the rest of my weekend?''

"Yes, of course I do,'' she said, smiling.

"Why is that funny?''

"Because you've been squirming for half an hour, and I wondered what you wanted to tell me.''

"This is why you're a reporter.''

"Right.''

"You really want to listen to this?''

"Really.''

I told her the whole Lucas Hecht story, and it felt so good to talk about it that I truly understood why people get hooked on priests, therapists, and other professional listeners.

"It doesn't sound so bad," she said when I finished. "I think you ought to call him back."

"But he doesn't really want me—I'm just a warm body substituting for a dead woman. A gorgeous dead woman, at that."

"How can you be so sure of that? Maybe it started that way. But that first night you were just grabbing at a warm body, too. Give him a chance to say whatever it is he wants to say. And don't be so insecure—at least consider that he might be genuinely attracted to you."

"Why?"

"I don't know. Ask him."

I thought about leaping to my own defense, listing all the things he might possibly like about me, but I was afraid the list wouldn't be long enough, and I'd just feel worse.

So I simply said, "I guess you're right. I guess I should call him back."

Sandra wanted to get back to work, and I wanted to see Charlie Barrington and make it to the university in time to catch Professor Hellman during his afternoon hours, so we finished our coffee and left. I promised to call and let her know what happened with Lucas.

My luck took a slight dip at Golden Age. Mrs. Schueller saw me come in, and she was free. I listened politely to the update on Kristin and her family, how busy they were, how well they were doing. When she began telling me how wonderful I was to visit Mr. Barrington this way, particularly in his time of need, I leapt in.

"Doesn't anyone else stop by to see him?"

"Not anymore," she confided, almost in a whisper. "Or at least, not on any regular basis. I think Mr. Woodruff says hello when he comes to see his father, although that doesn't happen very often. I don't think Charlie has many friends left. If he ever had any. But of course, I don't really know."

"That's right, I had heard John Woodruff was here. He and Charlie used to be friends—are they still?"

"Well, John is very friendly on his good days, but he doesn't have many of those. And I think it bothers Charlie that John doesn't remember who he is most of the time. So I don't think you could call them friends."

"John's room is close to Charlie's?"

"Yes, just two doors down, on the right. I'm sure he'd love to have a visitor. Don't let it bother you if he doesn't know who you are."

"Thanks, Mrs. Schueller—I won't."

Charlie was lying on top of the bed, dressed, watching what appeared to be Frankie and Annette cavorting on a Southern California beach. Must have been a classic.

I walked over to the wall and pulled the plug.

"Who died this time?" he asked.

"Almost me, Charlie, almost me. And I want some answers. I want to know what your connection with Castle Properties is, and why they might want people close to you dead."

"Nothing's my connection with 'em. An old buddy, Joaquin Meara, I think he has something to do with 'em. He helps me out sometimes, helped me find a place to live once. Nothing more."

Something had changed. Charlie wasn't afraid any longer.

"You gave it to them, didn't you? You gave them what they wanted from you. What was it? What was worth the lives of both of your daughters?"

"Nothing, I didn't have anything to give, I don't know what you mean."

He was plucking at the bedspread, and he started to cry. Silently. He wasn't sobbing or anything, but his mouth was working, and I saw a tear trickle down his worn cheek.

"Charlie, you don't have to give in to them, you don't have to let them win. You can tell me what it is, I can get them, I can make them pay."

He shook his head.

"Listen," I continued, "it's something that connects the four of you, isn't it? You, Meara, Woodruff, and d'Arbanville. Years ago. Isn't that it?"

He shook his head. Not denying what I was saying. Denying my right to know, maybe even my existence. He turned toward the wall, and I thought I might as well leave. But then he turned back.

"You don't understand, I know. You're young, and you don't think you're ever going to die. But I don't want to die, either. And if I can just hold on a little longer, Jesus will come back, and the Millennium will be here, and we'll all rise up to the Kingdom of God, all believers, and death will be banished from the earth. Joan and Lois, they'll rise up then, too. At least I think they will. They will if they were true believers. I'm sorry they had to suffer now, but it won't be much longer, and then we'll all be together again, in the Days of Glory. They'll understand, I know they will."

"Right, Charlie," I sighed. "I'm sure they'll understand why they had to die so that you could live."

"That's right." He nodded. "They will understand."

"Charlie—what if they don't come back?"

"Well, that'll be because they didn't believe, that's all. I'll be sorry, but it won't be my fault."

That was all I could handle. I turned to leave.

"Wait—miss—I don't remember your name."

I paused, hoping.

"O'Neal, Freddie O'Neal."

"Miss O'Neal, please plug the television set back in. The *Hour of Power* comes on at three, and sometimes it takes me a while to get a nurse in here, and I don't want to miss it."

The hell with him. I walked away.

I stopped by to see John Woodruff only because I was there, with no illusions that it would be a useful visit, which was a good thing.

Like Charlie's room, John's was a former double that had been converted to a single. And like Charlie, John was watching Frankie and Annette on the beach. It would have made sense to me to put them together, but maybe there was some kind of etiquette I didn't understand going on.

I rapped on the door frame.

"Mr. Woodruff? Could I come in?"

"Hello, of course, I'm so glad you stopped by."

He clicked off the television set at once.

John Woodruff was cherubic, that was the word for it. He was round and ruddy, with a halo of white hair and a smile that probably lit hearts when he was young. He was wearing a silk dressing gown and slippers. He gestured toward the only chair, and I sat.

"Now, what can I do for you?"

"My name is Freddie O'Neal, Mr. Woodruff, and I was hoping you could answer some questions."

"Yes, of course, of course. Delighted to see you."

"I was just visiting with Charlie Barrington—just down the hall—"

"Charlie—my God, how is Charlie? He's an old friend of mine, you know, and I haven't seen him in years. You spoke with him? How is he?"

"He's fine, Mr. Woodruff, just fine. He speaks very highly of you, too."

"Glad to know that. Now, what can I do for you?"

"I wanted to ask you about a real estate investment. Do you know anything about a firm called Castle Properties?"

"I'd have to look it up, miss, I'm afraid my memory isn't what it used to be. But if it's a local company, I'd bet on it. Nevada real estate only has one way to go, and that's up. I used to own some myself—I think I still do, but you'd have to ask my son, he's the one who keeps up on everything these days. There are a few areas that have problems with water rights—that's the only thing you have to watch out for—but if you have a chance to get in on the ground floor, buy in before the developers get there, I'd do it. That's my advice."

"Thanks, I'll look into it."

"Don't just look into it, miss, do it. Be bold, daring.

That's the only way to make it in the world. I used to be that way. Did I tell you I'm glad you stopped by? What can I do for you?''

I stayed until I could convince him—gently—to turn on the television. When Frankie and Annette burst into song, I slipped out.

Mrs. Schueller was on the phone. I waited for her to hang up.

''Was Van Woodruff here to see his father recently?''

''Yes—just yesterday, in fact. Why?''

''Just wondered. Say hello to Kristin for me.''

We exchanged bright smiles and I left.

There was a student in Professor Hellman's office, so I wandered around the basement hall reading the notices, newspaper clippings (with appropriate comments), and cartoons that decorated the office doors. A large handbill invited me to a birthday celebration for Benjamin Harrison, ''The Last Great Republican President.'' An obscure historical journal from an equally obscure midwestern college had sent out a call for papers on whether the opening up of Eastern Europe was indeed the End of History, as some scholar had posited. Two young men walked by, and I caught a bit of conversation about the role of slaves in ancient Athens, the cradle of democracy. Graduate school might be a good idea after all. Nobody slit fuel hoses in graduate school.

I saw the student leave, and Professor Hellman waved me in.

''You know,'' he said, ''since the time of Aristotle professors have been complaining about the decline in intellectual quality of the current generation of students, whatever generation it is, when compared with those of another time. And it isn't true, of course. The bright ones are always around—they are simply caught up all too often in the sea of mediocrity we all swim in. The young woman who just left is one of the brightest students I've ever had. You'd find her work interesting—she has some original thoughts on Robert Graves's *The White Goddess.* But will she continue her studies? No. She plans on going to law school! Another scholar lost to the world.''

''Law school is hardly a fate worse than death.''

''You aren't going to argue that society needs more lawyers, are you?''

''I wouldn't dream of it. One for every twenty or thirty Americans is surely enough.''

''Yes, well, you didn't come to discuss law or scholarship— although I wish you had, I wish our association had a more pleasant basis.''

''I do, too.''

I told him most of what happened, ending with Charlie.

''I can't ask you to continue,'' he said, shaking his head slowly. ''This has become far too dangerous. And if Charlie is no longer afraid, there may be no point.''

''Thanks for your concern. But now it's personal. I want to know who tried to take me out of the game. And I think Sandra Herrick can smell a Pulitzer here, and I don't want to disappoint her.'' I stood up to leave. ''Well, I guess you don't have much reason to see Charlie anymore, but if you feel like stopping by, he might be more talkative now that he isn't scared.''

''I never stop by to see Charlie. I never have. I saw him on rare public occasions, to please my wife, and I delivered my condolences on the deaths of his daughters, but I have never visited with the man and I do not intend to start now. Whatever bed he has made for himself, he can lie in it.''

''Ouch. Okay. I understand. I'll talk with you soon.''

Something was nagging at me as I left. I had been certain that Professor Hellman used to stop by to see Charlie. What had made me think that? The answer didn't come to me on the drive home, and then I forgot about it, because my rumination settled once again on Lucas Hecht.

Chapter
12

"ALL RIGHT," I said when he picked up the phone. "I'll listen. What?"

"Oh, great," Lucas groaned. "What a great start to a conversation."

"It's the best I can do."

"Look, it wasn't what you think."

"You were lovers, but it wasn't what I think."

"That's right."

"Then tell me what it was."

The only good thing about having this conversation on the telephone was that he couldn't see how hunched up I was, how shaky, how not wanting to cry.

"Joan and I were lovers, but it wasn't any great romantic thing, it was just sort of friendly. Built on mutual need. I was going through a divorce and a kind of midlife crisis about what I wanted to do, and Joan's marriage was rocky, and we both needed someone to talk to. That's all it was. We had no plans to run off together, or anything like that."

"Why did you both lie about it then? Why did she say she didn't have an alibi? She said she didn't know anybody at Echo Bay, and you said you didn't know her very well."

"Come on. Why do you think? Because neither one of us wanted it to get around. She didn't want to say that she was in bed with someone not her husband when somebody pretending to be her was killing her sister in Reno, unless it was really going to go to trial, and I didn't want to be part of a highly publicized mess. I still don't. In fact, that was the last time I slept with her. We agreed to end it.''

"How long did it last?''

"Off and on for a couple of years. Just when she was here, if we both felt like it. The relationship was warm and friendly and no big deal.''

"Are you going to say that about me, too?''

"I don't know what I'm going to say about you. Jesus, we don't even know if we have anything going yet. What do you want from me?''

That was a good question, and one I had no answer for. When I didn't speak, he went on.

"Look, all I'm saying to you is, I think I'm available for something, if you want to explore it. I do have some emotional baggage surrounding my ex-wife—I admit to that—but I don't think I have any about Joan Halliday. Her death bothers me, the way the death of anybody I knew well and cared about would bother me, and I'd like it if you found the murderer, if she was murdered, but that's it.''

"I need to think about it. I think I believe you, and I think I might want to explore this, but I don't want to do it right this second.''

"Okay. Call me when you do.''

"Lucas—wait—don't hang up.''

"Why?''

"Because there are a couple of other things I need to know.''

Silence. My voice had changed, I knew it had. I'm much more at ease when I'm operating out of my head. My heart calmed, my breathing was less ragged, I was back on the job.

"Could Mick have known about your affair?''

"I don't think so. Well, that's probably not true. He could have. We were discreet, but Echo Bay is small, and people had to know. Someone might have told him. The reason I doubt it is that I'm considered a local, people didn't even know Mick and I can't think of anyone in Echo Bay who would have butted that far into other people's business.''

''Was she afraid of Mick?''

''Not physically. If you're asking me if I think Mick killed her, I don't. Nothing she said to me made me think of him as violent. Neglectful, unappreciative, but not violent. She was afraid he'd ask for a divorce, though, and she wasn't sure if she wanted one.''

''I don't understand.''

I really didn't. This would have been an easier conversation to have in person. I wished I could watch it on a split screen, so that I could see both of us.

''You don't understand why she was sleeping with me and wanting to stay married to Mick?''

''Yeah, I guess that's it.''

''Well, I don't know what to tell you.'' There was a hard edge in his voice. ''It made sense to me.''

''Okay, okay, I'm sorry. You want me to tell you you're a wonderful lover, you are, I think you know that. That wasn't what I meant. What can you tell me about their relationship?''

He took a moment before he answered. His tones were measured. Mine probably sounded that way to him.

''She loved him, but she didn't trust him. She thought he probably saw other women. And he had something going he didn't tell her about. He'd be gone, and he'd come back with money. He said he won it gambling, she didn't believe him. That's it.''

''Mick said she was depressed. Was she?''

''Not that I know of. Worried—as she should have been, all things considered—but not depressed.''

''Her shrink said she had some kind of conflict concerning her father. Do you know anything about that?''

We were becoming colder and colder. Dissecting his relationship with Joan Halliday wasn't a good idea. I kept remembering that he had slept with another woman and lied about it. There was a nebulous line here, between what was personal and what was professional, and we weren't defining it very well. I wondered if there would be a personal relationship left to explore by the time we were through, or if the professional dragon would kill it, eat it, and defecate the remains.

"Only what you already know. If she knew anything about Castle Properties, she didn't mention it to me."

"Where were you when she died?"

"I'm not sure when that was. If it was on the day I met you, I was in the shop. If it was the night before, I was on the Second Chance. Alone."

"Did you hear or see anything that might have been someone going out to the Queen of Hearts?"

"No."

"Okay. I guess that's all. Do you still want me to call?"

"Yes. I still want you to call."

My heart was pumping pain through my body when I hung up the phone. I didn't know if I could trust him. I felt vulnerable, and I hated that. Sundance had crawled onto my lap while I was talking, and I had been scratching his ears without thinking. When I clutched him, he stopped purring and struggled to get loose. I let him go.

I was still sitting there, trying to figure out what to do next, when the phone rang.

"Hi, Freddie," a small, thin, child-like voice said. "It's me. Lurene."

"Hi," I responded.

"What are you doing?"

"Oh, just sitting here fretting about who killed the Barrington sisters."

"Oh. I'm sorry, I didn't mean to interrupt anything."

"No, Lurene, it's okay. You didn't interrupt. That was really a bad joke. Besides, I can fret later."

"Oh, good. The reason I called is that the play is opening tomorrow night, and everybody is inviting friends, and I wondered if you'd like to come."

"That's very nice of you. As a matter of fact, I would like to come."

"You can bring somebody with you, if you want to. I have two tickets for you."

"Thanks, but I'll come alone. Maybe you can find someone else to use the other ticket."

"Well, I don't really have anyone else to invite. I guess I'll just tell the box office I'm only using one. The show starts at eight-thirty, and there's a party afterward, in the basement of the theater, if you want to come to that, too."

"Thank you. I really appreciate the invitation. I'll see you tomorrow night. And break a leg."

Lurene—somebody who had fewer friends than I did. When I thought about it, and this was the second time in just a few days that it had been called to my attention, it was odd that I didn't have more friends. I mean, I had lived all of my life in Reno, a place where people know their neighbors. I had gone through Reno schools, from Mount Rose Elementary, to Billinghurst Junior High, to Reno High School, mostly with the same group, except for the year I skipped. I had somehow ended up knowing all of them, but made friends with none of them. I would have liked blaming it on my mother, but I couldn't figure out how to do that.

When I had received an invitation to my tenth high-school reunion, there was a flyer asking for memories of your best high-school moments with the gang. Pizza at Fontana's was suggested as an example. I had never had pizza at Fontana's, or not that I could remember. My memory has always been good for everything but my own adolescence, which is a painful blur. Someday I should probably see a shrink about it.

I didn't feel like going out—and I did feel like pizza. I called a pizza chain and had one delivered. I opened a beer to go with it, and spent the evening watching television with the cats.

The next morning didn't bring any new ideas—except an awareness I was sleeping in sheets so gray and dingy that the Marquis de Sade would have considered them cruel and unusual punishment. I tore the sheets off the bed and the towels off the rack (how many showers had I used them for?), and dumped the contents of the hamper. Everything fit into four pillowcases that I loaded into the back seat of the Mustang.

As I sat there in the laundromat drinking coffee and watching the clothes spin in the giant washer, I retraced every step in the case. Nothing leapt out at me, so I picked up a newspaper that an earlier riser had left on the bench. I was leafing idly through the pages when I saw the article on Van Gogh's "Irises," sold one more time. I tossed the clothes into the dryer, put in enough dimes to keep it spinning for an hour, and left.

Mrs. Lewis was wearing the same flowered apron over what I thought was the same housedress. She was glad to see me.

"I just have a minute," I told her, declining her offer of coffee. "My clothes are in the dryer. I just wanted to know—Charlie Barrington's nice son-in-law. Which one did you mean?"

"Mrs. Halliday's husband, the one with the red Corvette. He must've had business in Reno, to be here so often. And he always stopped by to see Mr. Barrington, every time he was in town. Not like the professor, Mrs. Hellman's husband. I never saw him, except once when it was Mrs. Hellman's birthday, and the three of them went out for dinner."

"About how often was Mr. Halliday here?"

"Not once a month, not that often. But more than his wife was, and more often than you'd expect from someone who lives in Las Vegas. Are you sure you don't want coffee?"

I declined again, and returned to the laundromat to retrieve my clothes.

That was one piece solved. I couldn't prove it without help from Mary Yates, which I wasn't likely to get, but that was the drug connection. Mick to Willie, Las Vegas to

Reno. And a reason for Mick to buy me off, whether he had anything to do with Castle Properties or not. The last time he gave me the check? Probably hubris, the same kind that causes men running for president to dare reporters to shadow them in search of extramarital affairs. Less likely— at least I wanted it to be less likely—was the possibility that he didn't think I'd be around to cash it anyway.

Handsome, shallow Mick, who was willing to allow his wife to be branded as her sister's temporarily insane killer to keep questions away from his business and himself out of jail. And then willing to let his wife's death be written off as an accidental overdose. He had to be connected to somebody besides Willie, somebody on the other end, somebody had to have talked to him, explained why all this was necessary. Somebody big enough, with enough clout, that Mick would go right along with it all.

Not Woodruff, junior or senior. Maybe d'Arbanville, junior or senior. Maybe the elusive Meara.

Clean laundry somehow made it important that I dust and vacuum and do something about the kitchen and bathroom as well. I went to the grocery store, too—might as well make a day of it.

Dressing for the theater meant a good pair of white denim pants, a new brown and white shirt, and a white denim jacket. For a minute I liked the way I looked, and thought about dressing up more often. I rummaged in the bathroom medicine cabinet and found an old lipstick. It didn't work. I just looked strange. I wiped it off my mouth and threw the tube out.

I drove to the theater, not willing to risk a cold, late night walk home, and got there about five minutes before curtain time. The small parking lot was already full, and I ended up parking about a block away. The narrow lobby was packed.

"Oh, good, Freddie, I didn't know you were going to be here," said a voice against my shoulder.

I turned to see Sandra Herrick and Don Echeverria. Anybody who blindly accepted the cultural bias that men age better than women do would have to rethink that position, with Sandra and Don as evidence. She looked stunning in a purple silk blouse and skirt and a white coat, slim and successful. He looked successful, too. But he had gained easily twenty pounds in the last ten years—and made the mistake of wearing a vest—and was already starting to lose his hair. He had a nice-guy face, with the jowls of an aging jock, and he was only in his mid-thirties.

"Don, you remember Freddie, don't you?"

He said something pleasantly noncommittal, and edged around so that he could shake the hand I held out.

"I have something for you—I was going to call you tomorrow," Sandra continued. "Let's just slide into the ladies' room for a minute."

The rest rooms were downstairs, next to a counter where coffee and soft drinks were available. A big tray of homemade brownies and chocolate chip cookies sat next to the coffee urn.

There was no one behind the counter, since it was so close to curtain time, but two women were waiting in the small ladies' room space where the mirror and washbasin were, so we stood just outside the door.

"Here's Hank Senior's address," Sandra said quietly, handing me a folded piece of paper from her purse. "Are you going to try to see him tomorrow?"

"Yes, I think so."

"Then let's do lunch on Monday. Did you talk with Lucas?"

"Yes," I sighed, "but I don't want to talk about him now. That can wait till Monday, too."

"All right. I don't really have to pee, so I'm going back upstairs. I'll see you later."

"No, I'll go with you."

We were rounding the curve of the stairs when she grabbed my arm.

"Hank d'Arbanville's here," she hissed. "I thought he'd be off campaigning somewhere."

"Maybe he's a theater fan," I whispered.

I had never seen him before, but I would have recognized him from his frequent appearances on the evening news. He was tall and impressive-looking, with a full head of dark blond hair. A large nose that had been broken in his UNR football days spread across wide cheeks and drooped over a neat, blond mustache that surrounded a small, mean-looking mouth. Heavy blond eyebrows shadowed his eyes.

The woman on his left was probably his wife. I had never seen pictures of her, but she ought to have been his wife. Stylish, but not too. Decorative, but not so much so that anyone would look at her instead of him. As the two of them turned away from the ticket counter, I saw the woman on the other side of him—Irene Rebideaux Martinez.

"Now I remember her," Sandra said, still whispering. "I didn't when you mentioned her, but now I do. Is that her husband?"

"I don't know."

As big as Hank d'Arbanville was, the man next to Irene was bigger. He looked like somebody's bodyguard. He also didn't look excited over an evening at the theater. The four of them entered the auditorium together.

My seat was about two thirds of the way back, on the aisle. A slender young man in a suit who also seemed to be by himself was sitting next to me. We glanced at each other and decided not to interact. The d'Arbanvilles and the Martinezes were several rows in front of me, also on the aisle. Martinez—if that's who he was—got the aisle seat, so his feet could stick out. Sandra and Don were on the other side. I didn't see anyone else I recognized.

The play really was a lot better than it had been when I saw that little bit in rehearsal. Van's voice still sounded too loud and too fake, and so did the actress's, but their timing was good, and everybody around me thought it was funny, and by the end of the first act, I was laughing with the rest.

I ducked out at the first act curtain, all the way out to the front of the building, because I didn't want Irene to see me.

I wasn't sure why, but it didn't feel like a good idea. Anyway, good idea or not, she saw me. Martinez turned out to be a smoker, and she followed him out to the steps. I would have taken a walk around the building, but our eyes met as she came through the door. Her eyebrows went up. I nodded. There didn't seem to be any point in staying outside after that, so I went back in.

The second and third acts, which were played without an intermission, both went without a hitch. Lurene was on time for her entrance. She was actually pretty good—she knew her lines, her timing wasn't bad, she looked vulnerable and appealing, and she was obviously having the time of her life. That's all you can ask in amateur theatricals.

Sandra caught me as I was heading down the stairs afterward.

"Oh, good, you're coming to the party. I was going to ask you at the intermission, but I didn't see you. Do you have a friend in the cast?"

"Not exactly a friend. But I had talked with Lurene—the maid—on a couple of occasions, and she invited me to come."

"That's right—the rent-a-car person. I haven't seen her before. This must be her first show here. I hope she stays, she looks good on stage, and she'll get better with a little experience. What did you think of Van?"

"A real heartbreaker."

"He's such a ham—I don't know how anyone takes him seriously."

The coffee and cookies had been removed from the counter, replaced by a spread of cold cuts, bread, and salads. The two people behind the counter pouring wine and opening beer waved to Sandra. She dragged me over and introduced me. I grabbed a beer before what appeared to be half the audience swarmed over me.

Someone opened the doors to the green room, where the actors sat when they were waiting to go on stage, and the party overflowed. Cast members started appearing in their regular clothes, some with stage makeup still on, some with that funny white look actors have when they have just scrubbed the makeup off. I saw Lurene and waved. She had changed into an oversize blue sweater and dark pants, but hadn't taken off her makeup, and was clearly on a performer's high.

"I'm glad you came," she said as she edged her way through the crowd.

"I'm glad you asked me," I told her. "The show was a lot of fun, I laughed, and you really looked good up there."

"Thank you."

She smiled. It's not always easy to say the right thing backstage—I'm not good at the Fernando ("You were mahvelous, dahling") routine—but I had evidently done okay.

"I wanted somebody I knew here on opening night," she continued. "I haven't lived in Reno very long, and then I didn't get to know the cast all that well."

"Except Van," I offered.

She blinked, and for a moment I thought she might back away from it, but she didn't.

"Yes. And his wife's here tonight."

This was not the place for confessions, so I grabbed her hand.

"Come with me. Sandra Herrick wants to meet you."

Sandra was great. She hugged and gushed and started telling Lurene a story about the time she had been in a farce that depended on timing, and what happened one night when a door stuck, and she couldn't exit. I looked around to see what else was going on.

Hank d'Arbanville was clapping Van Woodruff on the back, and both of them were laughing. Irene was smiling politely, and the probable Mr. Martinez was looking around the room as if he hadn't been listening to the joke. I dropped my eyes before he got to me. The woman I guessed to be Mrs. d'Arbanville was talking with a woman I guessed to be Mrs. Woodruff.

Someone sat down at the upright piano in the green room and started a medley of show tunes. The two stars of last year's production of *Oklahoma* dashed over to sing "People Will Say We're in Love." Everyone close to the piano applauded wildly, and after a whispered conference with the piano player, they encored with "One Alone."

"Next year's musical, Bud—*The Desert Song*," some-one shouted.

"Good idea, Daddy," Sandra echoed.

All in all, it was the kind of party that was only fun if you knew everybody, and I started feeling shyer and shyer as the crowd got louder and louder. I finished my beer, thanked Lurene again for asking me, told Sandra I'd see her Monday, and left.

When I reached my car, I stopped cold on the sidewalk and thought about checking for a bomb. I was going to dismiss it as a crazy thought, but I couldn't dismiss the tingle in my capillaries. I had to lift the hood and shine a flashlight over the engine. The grime looked undisturbed, so I crossed my fingers and turned the key. No sabotage. No bomb. I arrived home safely.

I hadn't looked at the address Sandra gave me, and I was surprised to discover that Hank Senior lived in Reno, not Carson—pleasantly surprised, because it would save me an hour round-trip in the morning.

In fact, I was knocking on Hank Senior's door a little after ten A.M. Like the Roberts Street house, this was another of the small brick houses that dot Reno. When I was little, and we lived in one, I thought the old brick houses were ugly. Now I find a certain square charm in them, with their predictable two-bedroom, one-bath layouts and their work-ing fireplaces. This one was on Larue, not far from Billinghurst Junior High.

The man who opened the door bore a strong resemblance to Hank Junior, although a little shorter and stooped. He also reminded me of the retired Lyndon Johnson—when he let his hair grow, like Buffalo Bill. Hank Senior's hair was white and swept back and curling behind his ears and down to his shoulders. His mustache grew down into his beard. White eyebrows bushed over the tops of glasses that magnified pale blue eyes. He was wearing a heavy lumberjack shirt and pants.

"What can I do for you?" he asked.

I handed him my card.

"I'm a private investigator, and a client of mine is considering making an investment in Castle Properties, so he asked me to make some discreet inquiries."

"You're lyin', girlie," he said, reading my card. "Nobody makes an investment in Castle Properties. But come on in."

I followed him into a room lived in by one old man with a lot of memories. The mantel was covered with framed photographs that overflowed onto the walls. But the dominant image was a portrait hanging over a leather couch, a portrait of a smiling woman in a lime-green taffeta evening dress, the kind with all the crinoline underskirts that was popular in the early fifties. She was blond and pretty and had to be Hank Junior's mother. The only place to sit besides the couch was a leather easy chair, which had been turned to face a very sophisticated sound system. This was a man who took his music seriously.

"Want some tea?" he asked, gesturing toward the couch.

"Yes, thank you," I said.

I ignored the couch to look at the photographs. The earlier ones were of himself with various people, some entertainers who had played the lounge of the Paiute Inn, some political figures, some people I didn't recognize. The later ones were of his son, with about the same mix. When I heard him returning, I sat. The couch was low, and once I had plopped into it, I knew I was going to have trouble getting out.

He placed a tray with a china teapot, two cups and saucers, cream, sugar, and lemon, spoons and napkins, on the low table in front of the couch.

"I was just gettin' it for myself," he explained. "That's why it's ready."

"You do all this for yourself?"

"If I don't, who will?"

His eyes smiled at me as he poured. He pulled the leather chair around, then sat and picked up his cup. He poured some cream, stirred some sugar, and leaned back. I squeezed some lemon and took a sip. The tea was something exotic, slightly smoky, that I didn't recognize.

"Have a cookie," he said, holding out a plate of Fig Newtons.

I didn't really want one, but I took it to be polite.

"So," he said, still smiling, "who are you?"

"I told you. Freddie O'Neal. I'm a private investigator. It's really true."

"Okay, I believe that. But I don't believe the rest."

"Then why did you invite me in?"

"Because you're a pretty thing—I was going to call you a pretty little thing, but you ain't exactly little—and I thought you might be good company for tea."

"I ain't exactly pretty, either."

"Sure you are, honey. You just need a little fixing up. I used to see the girls who sang in the casino lounge first thing in the morning, no makeup, and you'd be surprised how plain they looked—a lot plainer'n you do. So why'd you want to see me?"

"I really do want to know about Castle Properties, and it's because of something a client hired me to do. But you're right, he isn't a potential investor."

He nodded.

"And you won't tell me who the client is, but you was hoping to find a garrulous old man who'd be delighted to tell you the whole story."

"Something like that."

He nodded again.

"I might help you, I might not. First you gotta tell me what you know."

I told him some of the facts, some of my speculations. Sort of a sketchy outline of the case, leaving out what I didn't think would help my cause.

"Oh, hell, honey," he said when I was through, "you don't really think I'm going to help you tie my son to murder—or to organized crime—do you?"

I evidently told him more than I thought. Probably the way he kept smiling and nodding at me.

"No, I don't suppose you are." I set down my teacup. "It's been fun meeting you."

"No, wait, don't run off. Have another cup." He poured it. "Have another cookie. I like you, and I want to say something."

He also wanted to take his time about it. He poured himself another cup, added the lemon and sugar, leaned back, and smiled. This time I didn't take the cookie.

"See, I know time's catching up with us all. I know Nevada can't remain forever the last refuge of the free man, which is what it's always been to me. The place with no fences and no taxes. Where you always knew the man you voted for, from city councilman all the way up to the U.S. Senate, representative government just like it was meant to be when this country was founded. A place where a man's handshake was as good as his signature on the dotted line. I know it's going, but that doesn't mean I'm going to let it all go easy. My son and them other boys, they know it's going, too, but they think they can hold on to what they want of it. My son Hank's a friend of that California governor who's running for president next year, did you know that? Hank figures if he's senator, and his buddy is president, he can do a lot for this state. Keep the attorney general out of legalized gambling, pick up a few more jets for the Air National Guard, that sort of thing. I don't know if they can pull it off, but I think it's worth trying. I think this is a way of life worth preserving, at least as long as I'm part of it."

"And you think it's worth the lives of Charlie's daughters?"

"No, I wouldn't say that, girlie, and I'm sorry somebody decided it was. That just shows the whole thing's getting out of hand."

"Then why won't you help me put an end to it?"

"Because it's my way of life, and my son's career, we're talking about here. Listen, honey, it's time for you to walk away from this thing. You've done real well, but there's still a lot you don't know. And the more you find out, the more likely somebody is to decide you're no more important than Charlie's daughters. And I wouldn't want to see that happen."

I set my cup and saucer on the table and leaned forward.

"Hank, you have to understand something. I'm not going to give up. Somebody's already tried to kill me once, and I have to stop them before they try too often. Whatever is going on here, I don't believe it was worth the lives of your friend Charlie Barrington's daughters. And I don't believe it's worth my life. So I have to stop them before they take it. I think you could help me if you wanted to. If you don't want to, then you have to live with whatever happens."

He shook his head.

"You sure are spunky, and I admire that. I'll do what I can to protect you, that's all I can promise. And maybe if things work out, you could come back here, and we could have tea again sometime."

"Thanks. I'll look forward to it."

I shook his hand and left. When I got outside, I wiped my hand on my pants.

I knew where my next stop was, but I drove home first. There was no point in getting to Carson before night. I was out of luck in trying to get insiders to talk, so the Castle Properties files were next.

I spent the afternoon playing Risk on the computer, with Butch sleeping heavily on my lap. I couldn't concentrate on anything and kept losing the world. Twilight and a beer calmed me enough to eat. I microwaved some chili and watched the news. I was into flow-through mode, where the television washes through my mind and nothing stays—I have no idea what the pretty faces told me happened that day. About the time I was thinking of leaving, the phone rang.

"Freddie, have you seen Lurene today?"

It was Sandra, sounding worried.

"Not since I left the party last night. Why?"

"She's not at the theater, and the stage manager called her apartment, but there was no answer, and he tried her work number, but they said she never showed up today, so Daddy just called me and asked if I'd go on in her place with a script. I hoped you'd have an idea where she is."

"I don't. I don't even know where she lives. Do you have an address?"

"Yes, I got it from Daddy."

Sandra gave me an address in Sparks.

"Okay. I'll go over there and see what I can find out."

"Great. I have to get to the theater. Stop by and let me know if everything's okay."

"I will. Have you done this before—gone on at the last minute?"

"Yeah, I love it. See you later."

I took Second Street to 395 North, turned east on Interstate 80, got off on El Rancho Drive, and I was almost there. Lurene lived on Prater Way, in one of those small concrete-block apartment buildings built on a lot that originally held a single-family detached home. There were five apartments in the building, four the same size and a slightly larger one in front for the manager. Lurene's was upstairs in the rear.

There were no lights, but I knocked on the door anyway. I even pounded on the door. Then I walked down to get the manager.

Half of a wrinkled face showed through a crack in the door and one raccoon eye looked up at me.

"Yes?"

"I'm afraid something's happened to Lurene. Will you help me check out her apartment?"

"Lurene isn't here."

"Are you sure?"

"Yes—she's doing a play."

"She didn't show up at the theater."

"Who are you?"

"I'm a friend—I was called to come look for her when nobody could find her."

"Just a minute."

The door shut and reopened. A skeletal woman in her seventies, wearing jeans and a Sparks Nugget T-shirt, appeared with a ring of keys in her hand. Dead brown hair and heavy makeup didn't create an illusion of youth.

I followed her back to Lurene's door, which she quickly opened.

"See? She's not here," the woman said triumphantly.

I flipped on the lights. The living room had the kind of frail, plaid furniture that you find in motels. A cheap reproduction of a Braque still-life had been tacked to one wall. A pottery vase full of branches with dried pods sat on the coffee table. That was all I had time to notice when I heard a sound from another room.

The room was the bedroom, and the sound was a whimper. Lurene was lying on top of the bed, turned toward the wall, still wearing the blue sweater. But now there were brown stains on it, and I could smell urine from the doorway.

"Oh, God, Lurene."

She made another small sound.

"Oh, Jesus," the manager said. "I'll call an ambulance."

I put a hand on her shoulder, and something that tried to be a scream came out.

"Lurene, it's me, it's Freddie, it's okay."

Something between a moan and a whimper came out.

I moved to the foot of the bed and leaned forward on the

wall side, so I could see her face. It was a mistake. I had to turn away.

Whoever had battered her had been thorough. Both eyes were swollen shut, her nose was broken, her skin was funny shades of yellow and purple, and dried blood decorated the pillow with patterns like dead leaves.

I wanted to ask her who did it, but I couldn't. I ran out to find the manager, to find the ambulance, somehow to get help.

The manager was coming back up the stairs. I grabbed her shoulders and pulled her up to me.

"Didn't you hear anything?" I cried, shaking her. "Didn't anybody hear her screaming?"

"Stop that!" she snapped.

I let her go.

"No, I didn't hear anything, or I would have done something about it. And I think anybody else in the building would have, too. She's a sweet girl." Her face started to twist. "God, I could kill the bastard who did this!"

I took her hand and we went back in together.

Lurene hadn't moved.

I sat down on the foot of the bed and touched her leg.

"The ambulance is coming. And you're going to be all right." I had to say that. "Can you tell me who did it?"

The whimper again.

"Was it Van?"

The sound that wanted to be a cry. I couldn't tell if it was a yes or a no.

"Okay," I said, patting her carefully on the ankle, "just tell me when you're ready to talk."

We sat there, the three of us, in silence, until the paramedics arrived. Two very young men in white uniforms, one with a medical bag and one with a stretcher, came into the bedroom. Doris—the manager—and I moved away from the bed so they had room to get to her. The one with the medical bag leaned over her to check her heart and her pulse.

"Jesus," he said as he saw her face.

Lurene started making a thin crying sound.

"Is she going to be all right?" I asked.

"I don't know. Her heartbeat's strong, but I don't know what's happening internally, what's been broken besides her face."

They put the stretcher on the bed and rolled her onto it. She coughed, and blood came out of her mouth as they picked her up.

"Shit," the same young man said. "Could be a broken rib punctured her lung." He looked at the two of us. "Somebody's going to have to come with us, to check her in."

Both Doris and I volunteered. We followed the stretcher down the stairs. Doris stopped to get her purse, and we took my car to Washoe Medical. We stood lost in the hall while they wheeled Lurene into Emergency.

"Jesus," Doris said, lighting a cigarette. "What do you suppose happened?"

She looked for a place to toss the match, finally dropping it on the floor right under the No Smoking sign, and then sat on a nearby bench.

"I don't know. Can you tell me anything? Visitors?"

I couldn't sit. Hospitals make me edgy—the idea of being caught by the medical establishment, connected to the machines that won't let you die, makes me want to run for the hills. I paced.

"None. If she was seeing anybody, she didn't bring him home. It's a small place, and I would have known."

"Did she tell you anything about her life?"

"Not much. I knew where she worked, knew about the play. She had picked up in the last few weeks, started to glow, so I figured there was a man somewhere, but I never saw him. He was married, right?"

"Yeah, he was married."

"You think he did it?"

"I don't know. Yeah, probably."

"Scum. He's scum." She ground her cigarette under her slipper. She had forgotten to put shoes on. "You want to tell me what this is about?"

"No, not now."

A nurse with a clipboard walked over to us, and we gave her what little information we knew about Lurene. Which didn't include whether she had insurance.

"Look," the nurse told us. "Somebody is going to have to assume the financial liability here."

"Or what?" I growled. "You're going to refuse to treat her?"

"Well, no, we can't do that. But we have to know who's going to pay."

I grabbed the form and signed "V. Woodruff," giving his office address.

"How's that?" I asked.

"Thank you," she said coldly.

Doris watched her walk away.

"Whose name did you sign?"

"Her lover's. I don't know if he did it himself, but I know the son of a bitch is somehow responsible, and he can afford to pay for it."

We didn't have a lot to talk about. Doris was a retired waitress who worked part-time as a school crossing guard and didn't have much to say about her life. I had even less to say about mine. The silences stretched so long that we were becoming comfortable with them when the doctor came out, X rays in hand.

"The good news is that her lung wasn't punctured," she told us. "Her jaw was broken, and the blood was coming from her mouth. The beating was severe, but she'll recover. The bad news is that I don't know what her face is going to look like."

"Can we see her?" I asked.

The doctor shook her head.

"No point. She's sedated, and she won't be able to talk before morning. I'll have to report this to the police, but I'll tell them not to come until tomorrow. Do you know who did this to her?''

''No. Not exactly. It would have to come from her.''

She nodded.

''The police are going to want to talk with you anyway. How can they get in touch with you?''

I gave her my card, and Doris explained that she was the manager of the apartment building where Lurene lived, and the address was with the admissions nurse.

''Okay,'' the doctor said. ''That's it.''

I drove Doris back to the Prater Way apartment building.

''How do you feel about taking a look through Lurene's things—to see if we can find a relative's phone number, something like that?''

''Good idea,'' she said. ''Let's do it.''

Lurene's belongings were painfully few, just what fit in the closet and the dresser and the bathroom cabinet. I couldn't find any letters, any papers that would tie her to anyone. The few unpaid bills sitting on the dresser included a telephone bill, but there were no long-distance calls on it, no numbers to trace.

''Here's something,'' Doris said from the closet. She emerged with a high-school yearbook in her hand, from Chico, California.

''Thanks,'' I told her, taking the yearbook. ''I'll check Chico information and see if I can find a relative. Or maybe the yearbook will give some information about friends. Somebody.''

''Yeah. Good luck. Let me know if you think of something I can do.''

Doris locked the apartment behind us.

''Thanks for your help,'' I said as we walked down the stairs.

''Thanks for yours. The poor thing would still be lying there if you hadn't come over. Maybe for days, maybe till she died.''

I thought about that on the way home. Whoever beat her

up had to know she was in the play. Did he really think nobody would check—or did he know I would? Was the message for me?

The light was blinking on my answering machine when I got home.

"Freddie, where are you? You didn't come to the theater so I gather either you haven't found her or something's wrong. Please call me as soon as you get in, no matter what time it is."

I had forgotten about Sandra. It was a little after midnight, but she answered on the first ring. I told her about Lurene.

"Do you really think it was Van?" she asked.

"No. I'll bet he has an unbreakable alibi for every minute from the time he left the party to the time she was found. I'd bet on Martinez."

"So what are you going to do now?"

"Stop by and see her tomorrow morning."

"And then?"

"You don't want to know. I don't want you to be an accessory to a felony."

"Freddie, be careful. Don't do something dumb because you're mad."

"I won't." Maybe I would, but I didn't want to argue about it.

"Do you want me to come with you to see Lurene?"

"No, but if you want to, you might stop by later in the day. I think it'll just be you, me, and maybe Doris, and she's going to need some moral support. I hope they remember to take all the mirrors out of the room."

"And she might feel better if I tell her about the play, how much we miss her and want her back."

"Right. Are you going to finish out the run?"

"Probably. I don't think there's anyone else out there idiot enough to step in. Oh, God, I'm going to have to look at Van as if nothing's happened. It's a good thing I'm an actress."

"Okay. Listen, I'm all of a sudden exhausted. I'm glad you called me when Lurene didn't show. I'll see you Monday."

I was so drained of the ability to function that I gagged on my toothbrush and had the dry heaves, since there was nothing in my stomach to come up. But I got myself to bed, and the cats were there, and I finally calmed down enough to sleep.

Chapter

13

LURENE DIDN'T LOOK any better in the morning. She had been moved from Emergency to the Intensive Care Unit. Her jaw was wired, there was an IV feed hooked up to one hand, and her eyes were still swollen shut. Maybe the purple was a little faded, or maybe the yellow was taking over. She still looked barely alive.

"She can't talk," the nurse had informed me. "And you can only stay a minute."

She could hear, though. I took her free hand.

"Lurene, it's Freddie. Squeeze my hand once if you hear and understand."

She squeezed.

"Do you remember what happened? Squeeze once for yes, twice for no."

Once.

"Was it Van?"

Squeeze. Then again.

"Are you sure it wasn't Van?"

Once.

"Did you know the man?"

Twice.

"Could you recognize him if you saw him again?"

Once. Twice. A third time.

"Does that mean you're not sure?"

Squeeze.

"Okay. Sandra's going to stop by this afternoon—she went on last night with a script in her hand, but I know they want you back. I'm going to see what I can do to find the guy. And I'll check in again either tonight or tomorrow. In the meantime"—I stopped. What the hell could I say?—"heal, dammit, please heal."

Squeeze.

I had planned to break into the Castle Properties Office Friday night, steal the files, copy them at a self-service shop on Saturday, and return them Saturday night. Now I was facing a daring daylight burglary, because the self-service shops in Carson City wouldn't be open on Sunday, and I couldn't keep the files out on a weekday. Too easy to miss them. As it was, I was counting on Irene taking Saturday off. I didn't peg her for a workaholic—and I did peg her with a home office—so I had to bet that Saturday was safe.

I got a large cup of coffee to go from a fast-food stand and tore a small hole in the plastic top so that I could drink it on the way. I still managed to spill a glop of it on my jeans as I turned onto the freeway. The coffee took a few uncomfortable seconds to cool, and my thigh took even longer.

Since I wasn't sure whether anybody might recognize my car, I parked two blocks away from the small office building that housed CP Inc. I strolled casually up to the back door, glancing around the lot to make sure there weren't any cars I recognized. No Mercedes, no Porsche, but there were a couple of unfamiliar cars. Maybe one of the doctors was a shrink who worked on Saturday. Or one of the lawyers was working on a heavy case. In any case, it meant the door from the parking lot might be open.

I won the first ticket. It was.

The second ticket was going to depend on how hard the office lock was to jimmy. My guess was not very—I didn't think they were expecting me.

I won the second ticket. Locks aren't my strong point, but I have a set of tools, and I can handle the easy ones. Most of the old ones—and this was an old building, with original locks—are easy.

During my visit with Irene, I had noticed a large file cabinet, but no computer. I had to hope that they indeed had hard-copy files. I sprung the lock on the file cabinet.

I won the third ticket.

The next question was what to take. I didn't think anyone would be in, but I still didn't want to stay too long. I grabbed the files for Barrington, d'Arbanville, Martinez, Meara, and Woodruff. I grabbed Grant Deeds. I grabbed Agreement. I slid them into an old UNR book bag that I had brought with me, closed and relocked the file cabinet, slipped out the door, and walked calmly down the stairs, through the parking lot, and along the two very, very long blocks to my car.

I wanted to sit and read them right then, but I was too nervous. There was a self-service copy machine and photo service next door to the drugstore where I had bought the red stationery and the magazine. I had to wait while some poor soul copied three years worth of tax returns, and I was certain my nerve endings were emitting sounds like the violins in the *Psycho* shower scene.

The 7 files contained 192 pages, times 2 copies was 384 pages, times 5 cents a copy was $19.20 plus a lot of dirty looks from the two people who were lined up behind me. I kept smiling and nodding and listening to my nerve endings shriek.

I bought three manila envelopes in the drugstore, put one set in them, addressed them to Sandra, slapped what I hoped was enough stamps on them, and dropped them in the corner mailbox. That was my life insurance policy, in case anyone was waiting for me in the office.

As it turned out, no one was. I returned the files as neatly as I had absconded with them. The one thing I didn't know how to do was lock the hall door when I left. That was the last ticket, and the one I lost. There was no automatic way to lock the door. It had to be done with a key. If I was lucky,

Irene would decide she had failed to lock it when she left Friday, and put it down to early signs of Alzheimer's once she couldn't find anything out of place. If I was almost lucky, she would think maybe someone had come in and checked the place out but didn't find anything worth stealing and left, and she wouldn't think of me.

I stopped at Washoe Medical to squeeze Lurene's hand again, but she still couldn't talk, and I didn't have any more questions, and I wanted to read the files, and I hate hospitals, so I left quickly.

The files took me most of the evening, because I had to read and reread and piece things together, and there were still things I wasn't sure of. By the time I was through, I thought I had grasped most of the business, although I still didn't know much about the murders.

Barrington, d'Arbanville, Meara, and Woodruff had met in boot camp, in 1942. That was when they signed the original agreement, which wasn't much more than a Musketeers oath to take care of one another, to back each other up during the war. As it happened, they split up a few months later. Hank d'Arbanville was the only one who actually saw combat. Battlefield commission and a Purple Heart. Barrington spent the war as a communications officer at the San Francisco Presidio. Meara was with some kind of intelligence operation in Washington. Woodruff was an aide to Patton, but strictly behind the lines.

They converged in Reno after the war, not kids anymore. And while each appeared to be playing his own game at his own table, they had a little side game going among the four of them. A kind of insurance policy. In fact, a tontine. Winner take all. This was described in the second agreement, dated 1946, the one that formed Castle Properties.

This agreement specified a $1000 investment from each of the four, to be used to buy vacant land outside of Reno. That is, what was outside Reno at that time. There was also a complicated schedule of increasing investments over thirty years, all to be used to buy land. Anyone who couldn't make the ante was out of the game. Anyone who died was out of the game—unless by foul play. There was a murder clause. If one of the four met his death at the hands of another—even if the "other" was unknown, an intruder, a terrorist, whatever—that person's heirs got an immediate half of the company, reducing the shares of the other three. An incentive to keep each other alive. But ultimately, it was survivor take all. The last one of the four alive got everything. There were four signed copies of the agreement, one for each of the principals.

Hank d'Arbanville's wife had been the first secretary, the one who had administered the property. The original agreement on file in the CP offices was in fact Hank's own. When Mrs. d'Arbanville died, Irene had been hired. Both women had invested shrewdly. Castle Properties owned hunks of Reno, Sparks, Carson City, Las Vegas, bought over the years, and was probably second to the federal government in the amount of undeveloped land around the state it owned.

I could guess why having Hank Junior in the Senate would be convenient. He could pork barrel for federal water rights, for one thing, and he would have more muscle with local regulators for another. Water problems were serious in some areas of the state, and development strictly limited.

Things I needed to know: How did Charlie manage to keep to that heavy investment schedule during and after his bankruptcy? Why didn't they just cut him out? What was the deal? Who were his heirs once his daughters were dead? And, damn it all to hell, who killed them and why? After that came who fucked with my plane. But the wave that washed away the sand painting was who battered Lurene.

I had promised to call Chico information, and I did, with some guilt, because I should have put that ahead of the files. It didn't matter. If her parents were there, they didn't have a listed phone.

The yearbook didn't help much. Most of the comments written by her classmates were of the "You're so shy and quiet—I'm sorry I didn't get to know you better" variety. The kind I knew well. I found her picture, and the caption was only "Graduating Senior." No activities. She did look shy. Her hair covered half her face, she wasn't smiling, and she looked afraid of the camera. The only surprise was that she was older than I thought. The yearbook was twelve years old.

I put it down, another dead end.

What now? I wished that I had taken more files, and I thought about another foray. I didn't move after I thought about it, though, and I knew I wasn't going to do it. At least not then. It would take me a while to gather the courage to go back there.

Professor Hellman might know about Charlie's will. Although it wasn't likely, Charlie might tell me himself, once I told him how much I found out, or Sandra might have a way of getting access to the copy in the Woodruff, Wallace files, if there was one, and I would bet there was. Beyond that, I was too tired to think. I went to bed and slept until morning.

Actually, I slept until the pounding on the door woke me up. I had been dreaming, dreaming that I was fighting with a succession of faceless men, who were all laughing at me. Every time I thought I had hit one, he just disappeared, and another one took his place, like figures at a shooting gallery, or in a video game. Finally, though, I grabbed one and connected. I was hitting, and hitting, and hitting, and the sound became real, until the man faded and I realized that what I was hearing came not from my head but from the front door.

"Just a minute!" I yelled, reaching for my bathrobe.

I had been sleeping so soundly that I hadn't even been aware that my early warning system was signaling. The cats had left the bed and were sitting side by side in the hallway, staring at the door, ready to head out the bathroom window if someone came in they didn't like.

"Just a minute!" I yelled a second time, and this time the pounding stopped.

I opened the door to find an infuriated Deke on my porch, filling the whole space.

"Where the hell have you been?"

"Good morning to you, too. What do you mean? Where have I been when?"

"I been waitin' for you every night at the Mother Lode. Don't you think somebody's gonna worry when you don't show up?"

"Oh, for God's sake. Other stuff has been happening, that's all. I'm sorry you were worried about me. I don't suppose you brought coffee with you, did you?"

"No. I brought something else."

He stepped aside, and behind him stood Mary Yates.

"Hi," was all I could manage to say.

She nodded.

"Come on in," I said, gesturing to the canvas chairs. "If you'll excuse me, I'll put water on for coffee. And I'd like to get dressed. I'll be back in a minute."

I also needed to splash water on my face and brush my teeth and try to focus on being up and alert. I did this, put on the stained jeans and the shirt that I had tossed over a chair the night before, and returned to the kitchen. I made three mugs of instant coffee and took them with me to the office.

"Anybody need anything in their coffee?"

Fortunately, neither did. I'm not sure what I would have answered if one of them had. There might have been some sugar in the kitchen, but no milk.

"Okay," I continued. "What's going on?"

"Mary has a couple of things to tell you."

The canvas chair was straining to hold Deke. I hoped it would last for the conversation.

I nodded at Mary.

"I got to thinking about what you said, that Charlie's daughters had been murdered. I thought you were just looking to tie us into the drugs. But if it's not that—"

"It's not," I assured her. Not that I was happy about the drugs, but that was somebody else's job. You have to pick your battles in life, and stopping drug dealing at the Reno casinos was not mine.

"Deke told me you think it's all connected with Castle Properties, and that I should tell you what I know about it. I only know about it because of Willie's friend, Mr. Meara. Willie said Mr. Meara wanted him to come to Reno, that he had a place for me to live, taking care of Charlie, and that Willie could come, too. And if anything went wrong, all I had to do was call a phone number, and we'd have another place to live."

"I had figured Mick was running drugs to Willie. Meara was the Las Vegas source?"

"I think so. But all I know about Castle Properties is that was the name the answering machine gave, after Willie's friends got out of control, and trashed the house, and we had to find a new place to live in a hurry."

"Did Charlie ever say anything to you about Meara?"

"No—but I knew he knew him, because sometimes Mick would say something about giving him regards, but he didn't call him Mr. Meara, just a funny first name, like Walking. Walking sent his regards."

"Joaquin."

"That's it. I could never remember it."

"Was Meara paying you to take care of Charlie?"

"Some. Charlie paid me some, Mr. Meara paid me some. I think Charlie only paid me so nobody would wonder about it."

"Okay, thanks."

"You're not going to go after Willie then? I thought you might want to, but Deke said you wouldn't."

"No—and I hope Willie doesn't want to come after me."

"Yeah, that's another thing."

Deke had been smoldering the whole time, and I had known something was coming.

"When you tell your friends a story," he said, "you tell them the whole story. You don't be leaving things out the way you did with me. Not only did you almost die in the desert, you almost died in the goddam street. Next time you are in trouble I want to hear about it."

"I'm sorry. If I had thought you were going to find out anyway, I would have told you."

"And that's supposed to be fine with me?"

"Deke, it's the best I can do."

I walked them out, promising I would meet Deke within the next couple of nights. Neither Deke nor Mary had taken more than a couple of sips of their coffee. I didn't blame them. If I wasn't used to it, I wouldn't have finished it, either.

I puttered around most of the day, and in the late afternoon I called Sandra, to let her know what was coming in the mail and bring her up-to-date.

"How could you do that? How could you break in?" she asked.

"Because it was the only way to cut the Gordian knot," I said. "And because I'm hoping it will give you enough information to go public with the story. Once the story is out, I hope they'll decide it's too dangerous to kill anyone else."

"Like you."

"Like me, of course. But like Lurene, too."

"Oh, God, that's awful. I could hardly stand to look at her. Why do you suppose they didn't kill her?"

"I don't know. Maybe they thought they had."

"Well, they didn't. And when she can talk, they may be sorry."

"That's why as many people have to know about this as possible."

"Okay. So what you want me to do before lunch tomorrow is see what Don can find out about Charlie's will."

"Right."

"I might be able to do one more thing. I know someone on the Vegas *Gazette* who might know something about Meara. I'll call her in the morning."

"Good. How's the play going?"

"It's wonderful. I love doing it, although I'm completely wrong for the part. You know, I don't have the time right now to take six weeks for rehearsal and another three for the play. And if it weren't for Lurene—and Van—this would be great.''

"I hope you go back on television."

"Me too. Thanks. I'll see you tomorrow."

I hung up wishing Sandra weren't quite so up, so effervescent, so irrepressible. I knew it wasn't fair of me, to want all this to touch her more. She was who she was, and there was a lot of good in that. I wondered what it would be like, not to feel other people's pain.

And she did her job.

"All Don could find out is that Charlie made a new will right after Joan died," Sandra said as she slid into the booth the next day at noon. "To find out anything more, he'd have to break into the files, and he doesn't have your skills in that area. Besides, he's worried about violating lawyer-client confidentiality."

"Sandra, he probably has already."

"He thinks he's still in the gray area. Lawyers are good at that."

The waitress appeared, and we ordered. I glanced at the Keno board. I had lost.

"What about Meara?"

"According to my friend at the Vegas *Gazette,* he's old and fading. He had a cancerous prostate removed last year, but the word is that it had already metastasized, and he has a couple of months at best."

"Any children?"

"None."

"So with Lois and Joan out of the way, the only two surviving members of the second generation are Van Woodruff and Hank Junior."

"What are you thinking?"

"That Charlie's new will makes Hank Junior his heir, thinking that gets them off his back. He has no reason to leave anything to either of his former sons-in-law, nobody else really to leave it to, and Van wouldn't draw up a will making himself Charlie's heir. Once Meara dies, they get rid of Charlie, get access to half of Castle Properties immediately through the foul-play clause, the other half when old John buys it and Hank Senior collects. I wouldn't bet on John Woodruff lasting much longer, but Hank looks healthy as a horse. And they have to off Charlie, because he's one of those old guys who'll hang on until he looks like something out of *Tales From the Crypt*."

"Then Hank Junior becomes the sole heir. Why would Van agree to that?"

"Because he has virtually no shot at it anyway—the odds are against John Woodruff outliving both Charlie and Hank Senior—and because he and Hank Junior have doubtless cut some kind of deal. A new agreement, and one that wouldn't be in the Castle Properties' files."

The waitress brought our salads, and I waved a new Keno ticket at the runner.

"Why do you do that?" Sandra asked. "You're the only person I know who grew up in Reno who gambles."

"I do it because there is no Castle Properties for me to inherit, and playing Keno gives me hope."

"Okay. I won't preach."

"Good."

We both started to eat rapidly, then she pushed her salad away.

"I can't eat right now," she said. "I have to get back and start on the story. I'll get something down and then run it by Chuck. We're lucky he's an outsider—a Reno editor would never run it."

Chuck was Chuck Gillis, who had become the editor of the *Herald* a year earlier, when it was bought from the local owners by a national chain.

"I can eat," I said. "I have to fortify myself to go terrorize an old man."

She laughed, pulled a couple of bills out of her wallet and tossed them on the table, and left.

I put off seeing Charlie by going to see Lurene. I had no excuse for not stopping by the day before, except that I had dreaded it, and now I felt guilty. I felt really guilty when I saw how much better she looked. Better, of course, is a relative word. What I mean is that she was out of intensive care and in a regular room, with an unseen roommate beyond the curtain, her eyes were open, and she was propped up in bed. She raised her untubed hand and waved at me. I think she tried to smile.

"Hey, how're you feeling?" I asked with as much cheer as I could summon.

She shrugged one shoulder and reached for the pen lying on the tray across her bed. Someone had given her a pen and pad so that she could write her responses, either a thoughtful nurse or the police. In fact, if I wanted it, I had another excuse to put off seeing Charlie. Some officer I didn't know had called that morning to ask me to come in and make a statement. I had said I would after lunch. I didn't say how long after lunch.

Lurene pushed the pad toward me. She had written "Okay. Thank you."

"For what? For stopping by? I got questions to ask."

She shook her head and started to write again.

"Wait, if it's for finding you and bringing you in, you don't have to thank me for that. In fact, I'm not certain this would have happened at all if you hadn't been talking to me."

She waited, looking at me through a half-open right eye and a quarter-open left one.

"Okay, I'll back up. Do you have any idea who hit you?"

She shook her head.

"Do you remember at the party, the men talking with Van? One was blond, Hank d'Arbanville, and the other one was dark and looked like a bodyguard."

She nodded.

"Could it have been him? The guy who looked like a bodyguard?"

She made a series of question marks on the pad.

"You're not sure? It might have been?"

She nodded and waited.

"I think it might have been him, because he might be afraid of something you might tell me, about the case I'm working on."

She wrote and pushed the pad toward me. It said, "You think it's Van."

"I think Van might have had something to do with it. I'm sorry."

She shut her sad eyes for a moment. Then she made another question mark on the pad.

"Did he ever ask you whether you remembered Joan Halliday signing for that car?"

She nodded.

"What did you tell him?"

She shook her head.

"Did he push it?"

She nodded. Doing this as yes-or-no was a lot tougher than letting her talk would have been.

"Did you mention giving me a ride that night?"

She nodded.

"Was he upset?"

She nodded and wrote something. "Bad."

"Yeah, that's what I thought. So why did you ask me to the party?"

She wrote "Friend."

"With friends like me you don't need enemies."

I felt guilty and responsible and I wanted to cry. I had been pacing, caged between the curtain and the door, and I suddenly sat in the plastic chair beside the bed. Lurene held out her hand and I took it. I started to sob, wracking, convulsive sobs that knocked gouts of pain and fear and anger loose from my chest.

"This is awful," I gasped, "I'm supposed to be comforting you."

She just held my hand.

The sobs eventually subsided, and I finally got control again.

"Lurene—do you have any idea what Van thinks you might tell me?"

She turned her face to the wall. I waited, but she didn't turn back. This wasn't the moment to push it.

"One last thing. Is there anyone you want me to call, to let them know where you are?"

She shook her head.

I sat there as long as I could, holding her hand, but I had to get out of the hospital.

When I hit the parking lot, I didn't feel any better realizing that my next stop was another hospital. So I dropped by the police station.

The desk officer was a kid, maybe twenty-three, who managed to send me down the hall to the detectives' room with a maximum amount of officiousness. The only available detective, named Matthews, was in his fifties, wearing a white shirt that bulged over his belt, loose tie, and no jacket, and he looked at me as if I had ruined his day by showing up.

I explained that Sandra Herrick had called me when Lurene was missing because Sandra was a friend, and she knew I knew the missing person, and that was why I was the one who found her. That was all.

"O'Neal," he said, shaking his head. "You're a PI. You want me to believe it was a coincidence that you found her? Nothing professional?"

"That's it, sir," I said, looking him straight in his tired, bleary eyes.

"Well, if you discover anything more about this, coincidentally, let me know."

He pushed a card across the counter.

"You got it," I told him, pocketing the card.

My next stop was the Golden Age. No way to avoid it. But this time I was looking for Mrs. Schueller. I asked how she was and listened as long as I could to the response.

When I couldn't stand it, I broke in with, "Mrs. Schueller, do you know who witnessed Charlie Barrington's new will?''

"Why, yes, I did,'' she said, puzzled, because she had never thought of me as rude.

"This is awkward, but you don't happen to know what was in it, do you?''

"Absolutely not, Freddie, and if I did I wouldn't tell you.''

I had just killed Mrs. Schueller as a source.

Charlie was dressed, lying on his bed, watching television. I didn't have time to note the program, because he clicked it off as soon as he saw me.

"Don't pull the plug. It takes me too long to get somebody in here to plug it back in. What do you want? Who's dead?''

His tone was defiant, but he didn't seem otherwise upset that I was there. I was probably starting to seem like a regular part of his life.

"Your daughters are dead, Charlie, and we're going to talk about it one more time. And as long as we keep talking, I won't pull the plug.''

He nodded.

"You talk, then. I don't know anything.''

"I think you do. But let's start with what I know. I know all about Castle Properties except one thing: Why did they let you stay when you went bankrupt? Who paid your share, and why?''

"Why should I tell you?''

I walked over to the wall and picked up the television cord.

"This time it isn't just out of the socket, Charlie. It's out of the set. No TV for days.''

"All right, all right, it isn't that important anyway, and if you know part of it, you might as well know the rest.''

I dropped the cord and sat.

"Okay, Charlie, shoot.''

"Joaquin paid it. I did him some favors when I owned the casinos, so he wouldn't let them throw me out."

"What kind of favors?"

"If you repeat this, I'll deny it, you know that. You ain't wired or anything?"

"No, I'm not wired or anything. What kind of favors?"

"I just let him run a little money through, that's all."

"Laundering. You let Joaquin Meara launder drug money through your casinos."

"Just a little, just when he was first getting started. He was an old friend who needed a favor, and then when I needed one, too, he paid me back."

I thought of a lot of things I could say to him, but most of them had to do with right and wrong, and I knew they wouldn't make any sense to him. If I told him that he and Joaquin Meara were the reasons why the free enterprise system had to be regulated, he might have understood, but he might not. I decided to skip it.

"The first time I was here, you told me somebody might have thought you had something that you didn't have. Was that your copy of the original agreement?"

He nodded.

"Why did you think somebody might want to kill you for it?"

"No reason. Except it was the only thing I had that was worth anything. And some of what we did wasn't too legal, you know, and d'Arbanville, he wouldn't want it public. Young Woodruff had asked me about it, but as long as I knew where it was, I knew he couldn't kill me. There's that clause in it about murder, you know."

"I know. If you don't have it, where is it?"

He shrugged.

"I don't know anymore. I gave it to Joan a long time ago, sealed in an envelope with instructions not to open it unless I died under strange circumstances."

"And Joan opened it after Lois was killed, to find out why someone might have wanted to kill you."

"Yeah, she did. And I don't know where it is now. But it doesn't matter. The Woodruff boy told me it doesn't matter, that he'll take care of it if it shows up. He has his daddy's copy, and he knows all about it, so he said I shouldn't worry."

"Right, Charlie. You shouldn't worry. Of course not." Getting mad at him wasn't going to do me any good. I took a couple of deep breaths and went on. "I know you made a new will recently, and I think you made Hank d'Arbanville Junior your sole heir. Why did you do that?"

He worked his mouth around before he answered.

"You know so much, you ought to figure this one out. I don't have any assets to speak of, so it don't matter who gets them, until the others die and I get CP. And the Woodruff boy said it was only right that CP go eventually to the second generation of the group. He thinks I'm going to die, see. I told him about the Rapture, explained that I wouldn't die, so I wouldn't ever have to give up the money. But he wanted me to sign, and I did it to make him happy. I would have made Hank and Woodruff joint heirs, but Woodruff said it wouldn't look right, and none of us wanted people asking questions. Like you are."

"Charlie, you dumb fool, you're going to die just as soon as they want to get rid of you."

"Joaquin wouldn't let them do anything to me, and they know it. He'd get 'em if they tried."

"Joaquin has a couple of months to live, John Woodruff is out of it, you know that, and Hank Senior won't lift a finger to stop his son. As soon as Joaquin's gone, you are too."

He leaned back on the bed and lay there, staring at the ceiling, working his mouth. I fidgeted.

"What do you want me to do?" he finally asked.

"I'm coming back with a friend and a tape recorder, and I want you to talk."

Chapter
14

THE FIRST CALL I made when I got home was to Sandra, who was so excited when I told her Charlie would talk that I almost hung up on her. I suppose I should have been glad that somebody was having a good time here, but I wasn't. We agreed to meet at Golden Age the next morning.

The second call was to Mick.

"I wanted to let you know that the check is on its way back again," I said. "I can't accept it."

"What're you telling me, Freddie?"

"I know about your relationship with Meara. I ought to tell the cops, but I don't have any hard evidence, and nobody's going to go after you. Besides, since you have no excuse to come to Reno anymore, your days as a courier are probably over anyway. Let me just add, though, that if I see you up here, you'd better have a good story."

"Here, now, you're jumping to a lot of conclusions, unwarranted conclusions—"

"Can it. One more thing. Do you have Charlie's original copy of the Castle Properties agreement? Joan had it, and he doesn't know what's become of it."

"Why would I have whatever-it-is?"

"Well, you might think you could blackmail somebody, somebody like d'Arbanville, and that they wouldn't touch you because of your friendship with Joaquin Meara. If that's the case, I'd be careful, unless the copy's in a safe place.

Charlie made a new will naming Hank Junior his heir. I hear that Meara's dying, and my guess is that as soon as Meara's dead, you and Charlie are, too.''

The silence was so long I thought he might have hung up on me.

"Joaquin died this morning. I'm in your debt, Freddie, but I'll pay it off.''

I have a pair of custom-made boots that I only wear when I think I may have to defend myself or someone else. The toes are reinforced, and the left one has room at the top for a small semiautomatic. It isn't very accurate or very powerful—small guns never are—but it would be there if I needed it. I put the boots on and got the pistol out of my desk. I wasn't sure how soon the CP group would move, and I wanted Charlie alive until morning.

I had reached the car when someone called my name. I turned to see Irene Martinez walking calmly toward me, this time in a burgundy power suit with a pink blouse. I looked for the yellow Mercedes, but it was nowhere to be seen.

"Freddie," she said, smiling. "The most amazing thing happened. When I got to the office this morning, I found the door unlocked. My first thought was, little old forgetful me. But later in the day I noticed that some of my files had been rearranged, and then I thought, little old sloppy you.''

"I don't know what you're talking about, Irene.''

"Well, of course, that's possible. But I discussed it with some friends, and they thought it was time we all sat down and chatted about what's going on here. If you don't mind, we can take my car.''

"I do mind. I have other plans for the evening.''

"I'm afraid that doesn't matter," she said, still smiling.

"Irene, I could take you in seventh grade, and I can take you now.''

"Well, we're not going to test that. I thought you might feel that way, so I brought someone with me. Freddie, I'd like you to meet my husband, Raul.''

She looked at a spot over my right shoulder. I wasn't

going to fall for that, and didn't glance back, but then a high, raspy male voice said, "Hi, Freddie," as a heavy hand grabbed my right wrist and twisted my arm up behind my back.

I looked behind me and saw blue pinstripe. Not many men are big enough that I look them straight in the suit. A shadowed chin was even with the top of my head. I gauged the odds of breaking free, getting to my gun, and doing something lethal before they could pummel me into insensibility. I decided to wait for a better moment.

"Okay, I'm yours. Where are we going?"

"I told you—a chat with friends. How unpleasant can that be?"

I gritted my teeth and smiled back at her. Raul eased his grip on my arm, and the three of us moved toward a shit-brown Cadillac parked a half a block down. He pushed me into the back seat and climbed in after me. Irene drove.

The car was clearly not the place to make a move. I was jammed so closely against Raul Martinez that I could smell his minty breath. We rode in silence.

I tensed as we hit Virginia Street, but Irene went straight across. We weren't going to Carson. I had had visions of me trying to walk back to Reno from the house in King's Canyon. Visions of me screaming where no one could hear. Visions of them shooting me and burying me in the backyard. When we turned onto Larue, toward Hank Senior's place, I relaxed a little. We really were going to talk.

Irene parked across the street from the small brick house. Raul grabbed my arm above the elbow tightly enough that if I had tried to get out of the car without him, I would have had at best a dislocated shoulder. At worst, no right arm. I opened the door and we slid out together. Together, like old friends, we crossed the street and walked up to the front porch.

Hank Senior opened the door, beaming and waving like a gracious host.

"Freddie, so glad to see you again. Come on in, everybody."

He had moved three dining-room chairs into the living room. Raul and I sat together on the couch, and Irene took one of the dining-room chairs.

"The other two will be here any minute," Hank said. "I've made tea, but there's stronger stuff available for those that want it. Freddie?"

"Thanks, I'll take a beer. And I'd like to see the unopened bottle, if it's all right with you."

"No problem. Irene? Raul?"

Irene wanted a martini, Raul asked for bourbon on the rocks. The silence stretched while we waited.

"Here we are," Hank said when he returned, placing a tray on the coffee table. He had brought a large mug of tea for himself, not one of the small china cups of my previous visit. He handed Irene and Raul their drinks. I opened the bottle of Lowenbrau and ignored the frosted stein beside it.

"Now, Freddie, we need to know exactly what you know," Hank said, picking up the mug and settling into the leather chair. "You can start for us, and we'll fill the others in when they get here."

I was thinking about an answer when the doorbell rang.

"I just saw Van turn the corner," Hank Junior said when his father let him in, "so we're all here."

Hank Junior was wearing a tweedy sport jacket, slacks, and heavily tooled cowboy boots. Nevada casual, as if he had just been talking to the adoring masses. He was an impressive man, and one of the things that bothered me, looking at him, was that I probably would have voted for him if none of this had happened. He lost a little of his impressiveness next to his father, though. Hank Senior was clearly the brains of the outfit.

"Good, then we can all hear it from the beginning," Hank Senior told him.

Van came in, looking straight from the courtroom. They all exchanged greetings as if this were some kind of cocktail party, ignoring me. Van and Hank Junior took the other two dining-room chairs, where they didn't look too comfortable, and Hank Senior fixed bourbon and soda for both. Finally, five pairs of eyes focused on me.

"Where do you want me to start?"

"Well, honey," Hank Senior said, "there's a popular song that talks about getting down to the heart of the matter. So just tell us what you think happened to the two Barrington girls, and why you keep bothering us about it."

"Okay. First of all, I think you were all getting tired of not being able to touch any of the Castle Properties funds, except for occasional perks like low-rent housing. That none of you embezzled from the partnership required a special kind of honor, and I appreciate that."

Hank Senior blinked his soft blue eyes and nodded, so I continued.

"So here you were with Meara dying of natural causes, old Woodruff nuts, and Charlie turning into the Rotting Thing That Wouldn't Die. It was easy to conclude that CP was Hank Senior's by right of rational survivorship."

Both Hanks nodded. Van looked a little uncomfortable at the mention of his father.

"All you needed to do was get hold of Charlie's copy of the agreement, so nobody else could, and wait for Meara to die. Then you could take active control, figuring you could off Charlie, and Woodruff would die peacefully never knowing what you had done. Anyway, you had remained loyal in principle, and no one would ever know you fudged a little at the end. But Charlie wasn't as gone as you thought he was, and wouldn't give you his copy. So one of you killed Lois—I'd guess Irene in a blond wig—to scare him into thinking somebody was after him, and that he'd better give Van Woodruff—his attorney and his old partner's son—the agreement to keep it safe. He wouldn't do it—he'd already given it to Joan—and he told Van that. So someone talked to Joan. And you discovered Joan had read the agreement, and hadn't decided whether or not to make it public. But Joan could be gotten rid of—once you framed her for Lois's murder. You discovered Joan had threatened Lois, and that made it easy. You had forged Joan's signature on the rent-a-car agreement, but Van Woodruff, her attorney, and Mick Halliday, her husband, were both willing to swear it was her signature. You probably could have bought an expert if you needed one.''

I paused to sip my beer. I had to be careful before I went on. Nobody leapt in to fill the gap.

"You were never certain whether Lurene was observant enough to realize the woman in the wig wasn't Joan Halliday. For the record, she wasn't. And she really thought Van was interested in her.''

I paused for another sip. Van took a swallow of his own drink, and found the glass too fascinating to look away from it.

"Joan had hired me while she was trying to decide how to proceed, before she realized what she was up against—and therefore what I was up against—probably before she realized that people she had known for years had killed her sister. When I started asking questions, you decided Joan had to go before she got an outside attorney and blew the whole deal. I'd guess that one of you arranged to meet her on her boat. You came from Overton, not Echo Bay, and arrived after dark, maybe not alone. She told you to go to hell and you killed her.''

Hank Senior chuckled.

"Now how would one—or more—of us do that and make it look like suicide?''

"Everybody assumed suicide—or at least the people who counted did. What you're really asking is how one of you could have killed her without a trace, and the answer is, I don't know. Various poisons are possible, since no one checked for them. Smothering or strangling—it only takes six seconds for a strangler to cut off blood to the brain, and there aren't always bruises, especially if the victim doesn't struggle. You—whichever one of you it was—dropped the

Valium bottle by the bed, sprinkled some Jack Daniel's around, clapped a couple of good old boys on the back, asked them to hush it up for the sake of the family, and lo and behold, it was an accidental overdose.''

Hank Senior sighed. He put his mug down on the coffee table and leaned back.

''Well, girlie, there's a lot of guesswork here, and there's not a whole hell of a lot you could make stick with the evidence you've got—we're figuring you copied the files— but you could sure cause a lot of trouble. I was hoping I wouldn't have to say this, because I like you, but I'm afraid you're going to have to go.''

''Why? I figure you've got enough dead bodies around already, and you have to add Charlie's, so why do you want mine?''

I thought about reminding them that they'd already tried to get mine once, but decided to let the sabotage of my airplane go.

''What else are we going to do with you?''

''Buy me off—but make it good. Mick Halliday tried, but it wasn't enough.''

''She's lying,'' Irene snapped.

''No, I'm not. Mick paid me five thousand dollars to butt out. I took the money and kept going, because I figured if Mick was offering that much, it had to be worth more to somebody else.''

Hank Senior and Van exchanged uneasy glances.

''Why are you so interested in money?'' Van asked.

''What—you think only the upper classes want it? Did anybody here bother to check my finances, or how much I gamble?''

Nobody had. Fortunately.

''She's in the clubs a lot,'' Raul volunteered.

''Call Mick,'' Hank Senior ordered.

Van got up and went into the dining room. He came back with the receiver of a cordless phone in his hand. Mick had evidently answered. Van leaned against the wall as he talked.

"So how much did you pay her to fuck off? . . . Yeah, thanks, Mick, talk to you soon."

He clicked off the phone, turned to the group, and shrugged.

"Checks out," he said. "Mick says he paid her five thousand dollars, that she accepted the check."

"Okay, girlie, how much do you want?" Hank Senior asked.

"Fifty. I want fifty."

Hank Junior laughed, the first time I had heard anything out of him.

"Don't bet on it," he said.

"Now, wait, sonny," Hank Senior told him. "Fifty thousand may be better than another dead body. You're educated—somebody must have talked to you about moderation in everything, even if I didn't."

"He's right," Van said. "I've said all along that violence was not the best way to handle this. All it's done is complicate our legal position."

"Twenty-five," Hank Junior said.

"Deal."

I didn't want an argument over price. I didn't want an argument over anything.

"Done," Hank Senior said. "Now, about the copies of the files. Who'd you send one to?"

"What makes you think I sent one to anyone?"

"Because you ain't dumb enough not to. So who?"

"My buddy Deke Adams."

"Who's he?"

"He's a security guard at the Mother Lode—I wanted him to have a copy in case I got into trouble."

"What about Sandra Herrick?" Irene cut in. "We saw you talking to her. Why didn't you send her a copy?"

"I told you. I wanted to make a deal. I was talking to Sandra at the theater because I've known her since college, nothing more. If I'd sent a copy to Sandra, I couldn't have stopped her from going public with it if I'd wanted to.''

They exchanged glances, still wondering whether to trust me.

"Call him," Van said, handing me the phone. "Call your buddy. Tell him to come over here and bring his copy."

"He works graveyard. It's too late for him to do that and get to work on time. And if I insist, he'll think something's wrong. Suppose I tell him I've made the deal and ask him to meet me at my place in the morning?"

More exchanged glances.

"Okay," Hank Senior said. "Call him."

I dialed. Deke answered.

"Hey, old buddy," I said. "I just wanted you to know that everything's okay. They've agreed to pay, so I've agreed to turn over all copies of the files."

"Yeah?" was all Deke said.

"Yeah. So we're going to meet at my place, as soon as you get off work in the morning. I'll give them my copy, and you give them the one I mailed you, and they'll give me a check. I'll split it with you, just the way I said I would."

"Got it," Deke said.

"Now what?" I said as I clicked off the phone.

"Those who want to leave can," Hank Senior said, "except for you, of course, girlie. You have to stay."

No one made a move.

"Then I suggest a game of poker," he continued, "if you boys will bring those chairs back into the dining room. Nothing serious, nickel-dime-quarter, dealer's choice. Twenty dollars to buy in. Just a friendly game to pass the time. Excuse me while I put the coffee on."

I learned to play poker when I was ten years old, sitting next to my father at all-night games. It was probably the closest I ever felt to him. I don't play very often, so I still have the little-kid tendency to call games like Baseball, Spit-in-the-Ocean, and five-card stud with the hole card wild when I deal, which usually irritates the hell out of serious poker players, but Hank Senior found it amusing. It also amused him that I was winning. Losing didn't amuse either his son or Van Woodruff, however, and both were out of the game and gone shortly after midnight. A grandfather clock with a muffled gong had squeaked the hour.

Irene folded about one-thirty and headed for the guest bedroom. Raul fell asleep on the couch about three.

Hank Senior and I were both so wired on black coffee that I knew we were good until dawn.

If I had been a smart person, I would have lost my twenty early, and either slept so my wits would be sharp in the morning, or figured out a way to escape. But I got caught up in the game, and I had to play to win. I think part of me was afraid it was the only way I was going to beat him. If he had me killed in the morning, I was still going to beat him at poker.

Sometime around four-thirty, when I was starting to slowly lose what I had won earlier, I thought about trying to escape, but I didn't. If I had pulled my gun, Hank Senior would probably have dared me to go ahead and shoot, and I'm not sure I would have done it. Even if I shot him, the sound would have awakened Raul and Irene, and then I would have had to shoot them. Disabling or murdering three people—with a small handgun—didn't feel like a good thing to try. If there was another way to get out of there, I was too far gone to figure it out.

We played until the light was full, neither one of us gaining a real advantage. I'm not that good, and over time he would have taken me, but about five-thirty I had started a new run of luck. When my father used to tease me about being lucky at cards, unlucky at love, I fantasized about growing up to be a glamorous riverboat gambler, wearing a black, full-skirted evening dress, with dyed ostrich plumes in my hair, going back to my small room alone each night after the game. And here I was, the reality, in jeans and workshirt, wanting to go home alive.

I had just won a big pot—I really did have the flush, and

he thought he could bluff me out of it—when Hank Senior said, "Pretty good, girlie. We got to quit for now, but I hope we can do this again sometime."

I counted up my chips, and he gave me $82.70 out of his pocket. He woke Raul, poured him coffee, and then finished cleaning up the chips, cards, and coffee cups. I looked at the grandfather clock. It was a little past seven. They were going to get me to my place before Deke had a chance to get there and set something up. And I was too tired to think of a way to delay them.

Irene came into the dining room looking mussed and unhappy, and got herself a cup of coffee.

Hank Senior walked in with a check in one hand and a pen in the other.

"Here," he said to Irene. "Sign this."

She did, and he handed me a CP Inc. check for $25,000. He had already signed it. Of course. Hank Senior was the vice president, not Hank Junior. Sloppy of me not to have thought of that before.

Hank Senior waved good-bye to us from the porch, the thoughtful host to the last. Raul had my arm again. Irene stumbled as she walked down the front steps.

"Are you sure you want to drive?" I asked politely.

She just glared.

Irene drove slowly and carefully. Larue to Arlington, Arlington to California, California to Virginia. We would be at my house by quarter to eight, and there was no way I could expect Deke before eight-fifteen. I was almost certain that he wouldn't walk in without a plan, but the delay almost could kill both of us.

I turned the key and opened the front door, Raul still at my elbow. I crossed the threshold just ahead of him, but he suddenly stopped cold and let out a kind of squeal. He dropped my arm and started flailing his hands as he stood there. Irene rushed up to him.

"What's the matter?" she cried.

"Get away from him," said Deke's voice, coming from

the porch behind her. "And you, asshole, don't struggle. You'll strangle yourself."

Deke pushed Irene inside and came in after her. Raul stood there and flailed for a moment, but then he quieted down.

When I stepped into my office, I could see the wires. Deke had rigged a wire noose over the door, like a rabbit trap, but the triggering wire ran out the side window. He had watched us enter, so he could drop the noose at the right time on the right person.

"Oh, God, Deke, thanks. I was afraid you wouldn't be here yet. How did you get off work so early?"

He glared at me.

"How do you think? I called in sick right after I talked to you. I been here all night. I didn't know just who or what was coming—you didn't tell me a lot on the phone—and I couldn't risk anybody getting here before I was ready for them. Copy of whatever, indeed. What else don't I know about?"

"I don't know. I can't think. I'll tell you the rest of it when I can."

The reality of the changed situation crashed upon Irene. She let out a primal war cry and charged at me. I grabbed her right arm and jerked her past me, then I got her with my boot in the back of the knee. She thunked onto her kneecaps. I was sort of hoping she'd get up and charge me again, but she didn't.

I really wanted to hit her.

Chapter
15

THE POLICE, THE courts, and the attorneys took over at that point, and cleaning it all up took months. I charged Raul and Irene with kidnapping, but I ended up dropping the charges, in exchange for which Irene dropped a breaking and entering charge against me, for the raid of the CP files.

I didn't make it to the Golden Age that morning, but Charlie talked to Sandra anyway. The *Herald* ran the story, and Sandra did win a Pulitzer. KRNO offered her anything she wanted to come back, but she decided to stay with the paper after all.

Sandra's moving account of Lurene's battering attracted a lot of sympathy that translated into the money to pay for plastic surgery to restore her face. She became active in the Reno Theatrical Society, and every time I saw her on stage, she looked fantastic.

Van Woodruff and the d'Arbanvilles sued the *Herald* for libel, but the suit was settled out of court with a sealed decree. A blue ribbon grand jury of long-time Nevadans investigated and decided there wasn't enough evidence to indict anyone. Nevertheless, the Nevada Gaming Commission—the one group that, even over time, appeared to be immune to the genteel amorality that permeated the state—pulled the Paiute Inn license and barred all of the principals from the industry. Hank Junior decided not to run for the Senate after all.

The FAA ruled that my Cherokee had been messed with by person or persons unknown.

Mick Halliday ran his red Corvette into a cement wall late one night and was killed instantly. Nobody investigated. I read about it in the paper and I turned the page. I wouldn't have thought about him again, but the day after he died, Charlie's copy of the CP agreement arrived in the mail.

I went to Golden Age to see Charlie, to let him know I had it and offer it back. He told me to keep it and said he'd make me his heir, but it wouldn't mean anything because he wasn't going to die anyway. He's such a tough old bastard I almost believed him.

I had mailed back Mick's check and turned over the CP one as evidence, and I didn't even want to think about how much I was out on the job. I stopped by to turn in a report to Professor Hellman. He thanked me, and asked again if I wanted to go to graduate school. I didn't.

I didn't call Lucas Hecht. He called me, when he flew to Reno to testify before the grand jury. I had dinner with him, mostly because I couldn't figure out what else to say when he called.

Whatever had happened between us wasn't there anymore. I had known that, even before I saw him.

The original flash of attraction with Lucas was probably something like what happens to actors on location, or accountants on a New Year's Eve audit: You're together, and the thing you're sharing isolates you from everyone else, and the sharing turns into passion. When I saw him six months later, he just looked like one more geographically undesirable, overweight, middle-aged Peter Pan. I looked for whatever it was in him that had inspired lust, and I couldn't find it. In fact, he looked so unattractive in his plaid shirt and jeans that I was embarrassed I had ever gone to bed with him. It was inappropriate, dammit—whatever your dropout politics, you wear a suit if you want the grand jury to take you seriously. I was glad I hadn't mentioned him to Deke.

For a couple of months, I thought I was going to lose Deke. Stephanie thought she was pregnant again, and Deke was determined to do the right thing if she was. She wasn't pregnant, and he really knew that marrying her wasn't the right thing.

One day in April I flew to Tonopah to have the promised beer with Paul. He had read the whole story by then, and so had everyone else in Tonopah, so I was a minor celebrity for a few hours. It was kinda fun.

The night after I said good-bye to Lucas, I wandered down to the Mother Lode for dinner. Deke was sitting at the counter, cutting up his steak. He glanced sideways at me out of red-rimmed eyes.

"You here again?" he asked. "What's the matter, don't you have any friends?"

"I love you, too, Deke," I said.

I ordered a beer from Diane and flagged down the Keno runner. You never know when you're going to get lucky.